Shandra Higheagle Mystery Series

Double Duplicity

Tarnished Remains

Deadly Aim

Murderous Secrets

Killer Descent

Tarnished Remains

A Shandra Higheagle Mystery

Paty Jager

TARNISHED REMAINS: A Shandra Higheagle Mystery
Copyright © 2015 Patricia Jager

Contact Information: info@windtreepress.com

Windtree Press
Beaverton, Oregon

Visit us at http://windtreepress.com

Cover Art by Christina Keerins

Published in the United States of America
ISBN 9781940064949

Dedication

This book is dedicated to my mom, Regina Norman, for understanding my love of reading and ordering the whole Nancy Drew set of mysteries for me to read as a child. She started my love of mystery books. I wish you could see where my love of reading has led me.

Chapter One

Shandra Higheagle leaned on the shovel handle, staring into the pine forest to her right. She loved her excursions up Huckleberry Mountain to collect clay. She'd purchased this land two years ago for this pocket of clay. The yellowish mud, when cleaned and purified, enhanced her art. Using Mother Nature's bounty to make her inspirations come to life enriched the overall appearance and authenticity of her work. That she used natural clay and formed pottery as her ancestors once had, made her pieces unique and sought after.

Enough musing and wasting time. She raised the shovel, sunk the metal blade into the ground six inches, and pulled out a shovel full of yellow clay. The packed soil held enough moisture to cling to the shovel. She knocked the blade against the top of the bucket, dropping the clay in. A good shove with her foot set the spade into the ground for another scoop. The metal grated on something hard; possibly a rock. She'd hit a few while digging clay in this pocket.

Wiggling the shovel, she shoved again and pulled up another chunk of clay. Her artistic imagination saw a chunk on the side that resembled the shape of a cowboy boot heel. Shandra chuckled at her imagination and knocked the shovel against her plastic bucket. The chunk broke apart and a boot heel fell to the outside of the bucket.

Shandra eased down onto her knees beside the bucket. Using her trowel, she broke up the rest of the chunk. Nothing.

Perhaps someone—years ago—while riding or hiking up here lost a boot heel.

She stood, picked up the shovel, and sunk the blade into the ground not far from the last scoop.

Instead of the usual high pitched zing of the metal slicing through the soil, there was the sound of a stick breaking. She shoved the blade farther with her booted foot. Another crunch, and she shoved down on the handle, freeing a section of clay larger than her usual scoopful.

Tingles raced up her spine at the sight of something white sticking out of the clay. She lifted and tipped the shovel, dumping the clod on the ground.

Her dead Nez Perce grandmother's face flashed through her mind.

"Ella, what have I stumbled onto?" Shandra asked her grandmother.

She picked up her trowel and knelt beside the chunk of clay. Slow, small cuts with the trowel soon revealed she'd dug up a leather cowboy boot with intricate detailing and the foot it encased.

She'd made a thorough search of all the Native American burial grounds before purchasing this ranch on Huckleberry Mountain. There wasn't any record of an Indian burial ground on the property. She'd made certain. With that information, and seeing the detail on the boot, she was pretty sure this wasn't an Indian.

Reaching into her back pocket, Shandra slid her cell phone out. One faint bar of coverage up here.

Nine-one-one or Detective Ryan Greer?

Admitting to herself she wouldn't mind seeing the detective again, she punched in his number. They'd met a month ago when she'd been a suspect in a gallery owner's murder. They'd come away from the event friends. She also wasn't shy to admit, she'd like to explore her friendship with the handsome detective a little more. They'd spent several days after his last case in Huckleberry talking, riding horses, and getting to know more about one another. She hadn't heard from him in several weeks.

"Detective Greer."

"Ryan, it's Shandra Higheagle—"

"Shandra, I've been meaning to call you. Work has been dragging me out in the early hours and dropping me into bed close to midnight."

She smiled at his boyish need to explain why he hadn't called. "I'm afraid I'm going to add to your work."

"Don't tell me you found another dead body," he said in a joking tone.

"I'm afraid I did."

"Where? Are you in danger?" His demeanor went from joking to all business.

The sound of tires dragging against gravel proved he was out in his SUV somewhere in Weippe County.

"I'm on my property digging clay. No, I'm not in danger. This person looks to have been here a while." She gave him all the details.

"I'll be there in an hour. Don't do any more digging."

His siren shrilled in the background.

"Go to the ranch and have Lil bring you up."

"Will do."

Shandra closed her phone and stared down at the bone and the leather boot. "Who are you and why are you on this mountain?"

Even though Ryan told her not to dig any more, her curiosity got the better of her. At least she'd read enough about archeological digs and even helped out at one in high school to know to use her hands and go slow to not damage any evidence.

In the time it would take Ryan to get here, she could have something more than a foot and boot for him to investigate.

~*~

Ryan pulled into Shandra's ranch, his siren still shrieking and lights flashing. The serene cabin and studio in the middle of the forest made him feel like an interloper. He switched off the lights and siren immediately and then the engine.

Crazy Lil, Shandra's hired hand, approached the car with a scowl. "What you scarin' all the animals for?"

Ryan stepped out of the vehicle. Crazy Lil's head came to the middle of his chest. For a small woman she gave off a larger presence. He knew little about the woman other than she worked for Shandra Higheagle and all the locals called her Crazy Lil—but not her employer.

He'd met Shandra under the worst of circumstances a month ago when an overzealous newbie tried to arrest her for murder when she was found in the same room as a recently murdered gallery owner.

His heart picked up pace remembering his first encounter with the intriguing woman and the days they spent together after he solved the case.

"Wanna wipe that grin off your lips and tell me why you came screaming in here?" Crazy Lil smacked him in his solar plexus, causing air to whoosh between his teeth and lips.

"There's no need to hit an officer of the law," he snapped, rubbing his chest. "Shandra called. Said she found a body and wanted me to come check it out."

The woman's face paled. "A body?"

"Yes. She said to have you bring me to her. She found it where she collects clay." Ryan waved to the passenger side of his SUV. "Hop in."

Crazy Lil shook her head. "Can't get there with a vehicle. Have to ride a horse."

"How does Shandra bring down the clay?" He

knew the woman was tenacious, but he couldn't see her packing buckets of clay off the mountain.

"She's got horses." Crazy Lil rolled her eyes and turned toward the barn and corrals. "You can ride Oliver." She whistled.

One horse trotted to the corral railing and hung his head over. He had some age on him judging from the gray in his red coat and the sway in his back. Ryan might have worked in the big city of Chicago, but he grew up on a ranch forty miles from this mountain. He knew horses, and he knew how to ride.

"I don't think that sorrel will make it up the mountain without someone on his back. Let alone carrying me." He waited for a response from the woman.

She spun about. "You gonna talk or you gonna help me saddle up the horses?"

Ryan studied the woman marching into the barn. She was either an ornery, abrupt, no-nonsense person or socially inept. Given what Shandra had said about the woman growing up on the ranch and rarely leaving, he'd go with socially inept.

He hustled into the barn behind the woman and was relieved to see two younger, spryer geldings in stalls. One was the horse he'd rode when Shandra gave him a tour of her property.

"Do I get Duke? He and I got along fine the last time I rode him." He walked to the stall with the bay horse, hanging a wide, white-blazed face over the gate.

"You might as well, you aren't riding my

horse." Crazy Lil pointed to a saddle hanging over a stand. "Use that one."

Ryan picked up the halter hanging by Duke's stall and opened the gate. "Hey boy, remember me?"

Fifteen minutes later, Ryan had Duke tacked up and his gear stowed on the saddle. He threw a leg over his mount and followed Crazy Lil up the side of the mountain. This was his first trek into the mountains for a body. He hoped whatever Shandra had stumbled into didn't get her caught up in trouble. The woman seemed to be a magnet for murder.

Chapter Two

Sheba, her large, black dog with a cowardly-lion's heart, started woofing and within minutes Shandra heard the creak and jingle of horses approaching. She shoved the loose strands of hair back from her face and stood. She'd managed to uncover another boot and move enough clay to show two leg bones. The body had been here for quite some time. She found it curious that she hadn't uncovered any information about a missing person in this area.

Shandra watched her oversized dog bound toward the horses and riders. Ryan called out to the dog, causing the animal to roll onto her back and whimper like a puppy.

Shandra laughed at the antics of her pony-sized dog.

Lil and Ryan stopped their horses beside the two she'd brought up. Apple, her appaloosa, who she rode, and Sammy, a gelding, she used to pack the buckets of mud.

Ryan dismounted and strode toward her. His eyes held hers before skimming down her denim shirt covering a turquoise tank and on down her denim pants and riding boots.

"Do you always gather this much clay on yourself when collecting?"

The teasing tone and glint of mischief in his eyes made her smile.

"Usually, I don't dig with my hands." She held up her yellow tinged hands with clay stuck under her short nails.

"Why were you digging?" He pivoted and found her excavation work. Swinging back around, his gaze wasn't as welcoming. "I told you not to dig anymore. You could have disturbed evidence."

"I didn't. I was careful. One summer I worked as a lackey at an excavation site not far from my step-father's ranch. I know not to mess with the bones."

A horse snorted and that's when she noticed Lil still sitting on her horse. The woman's face was white and her head moved back and forth as if denying something.

"Lil?" Shandra headed toward the woman and the horse. "Lil?" She reached up, touching the woman's leg. "Lil, are you okay?"

"It can't be," Lil muttered and swung her horse around, racing off through the trees.

"That was strange," Shandra commented,

looking back at Ryan.

"They do call her 'Crazy' Lil." He knelt by the bones she'd uncovered. "Tell me how you found these."

Shandra repeated how she'd been digging and pulled up a scoop of clay to discover it was a boot with the bones still inside.

Ryan nodded. "This has been here a while. There's no flesh, only bone. In this air-tight, moist environment it would have taken the flesh longer to deteriorate."

"Any idea how long ago?" She peered down at the bones she'd uncovered.

"Nope. I'll call in someone to exhume the body and get it to the state forensics lab." He held his phone in the air.

"You'll be lucky if you get one bar."

"I shouldn't leave this alone now that it's been found." Ryan peered down at the bones.

"Try my phone, it's configured with the towers around here." She pulled her phone out of her back pocket and held it out.

Ryan accepted her phone. She didn't appear to want to leave the site any more than he did. He'd wanted to call and ask her out on a date. There were only a couple months left until his brother married Ryan's ex-girlfriend. He wanted to arrive at the wedding with Shandra on his arm more than he'd wanted to get away from sheep ranching and the small community where he grew up.

He punched in the number of the Weippe County Sheriff's Department. "Hi Cathleen. I need to speak to Sheriff Oldham.”

"You find a date for Conor’s wedding?”

This personal knowledge and conversation at work was the downside of having a sister who worked at county dispatch. Ryan groaned. “Why is everyone worried about me having a date for the wedding? It’s still a couple months away.”

"This isn’t your phone you’re calling from.”

Tapping and clicking sounded through the phone. “Sis, don’t you dare—”

"Shandra Higheagle is letting you use her phone for business? What’s up? And don’t leave out any of the tiny details.”

"Nothing is up. Ms. Higheagle found a body on her premises. I’m trying to tell the sheriff.”

"Why didn’t you say so? I’ll put you right through.”

Ryan squeezed his eyes closed and slapped his hat against his thigh. Sisters. He had two of the nosiest.

"Detective Greer, I hear you have a body?” Sheriff Oldham was getting close to retirement, but he loved his job and made sure everyone around him did too.

"It could just be an accidental death. The body was found buried in clay on Huckleberry Mountain by a citizen. The body appears to have been on the mountain for some time. We’ll need a team to exhume the remains without disturbing evidence.” He shot a glance at Shandra who didn’t appear the least bit ashamed for having uncovered more than a layperson should have.

"It’ll take some time to get a crew together.

How remote is the site?"

"It's on private property and requires horses to get to it." Ryan scanned the area. "There's a slight chance a good chopper pilot could get in."

Oldham grunted. "What's your thoughts on the best way to extract the body?"

"Bring in a crew on horseback. Once they have it ready to transport call in a chopper to lift it out." This wasn't the first time the sheriff had asked his thoughts on a problem. Cathleen had been dropping hints the sheriff thought Ryan would make an excellent replacement when he retired.

"Do you feel confident in leaving the site to escort the team into it? And where should I have them meet you?" The sheriff was old-school.

Ryan heard a pen scratching across the ever-present note pad on the sheriff's desk.

"Only three of us know about the body. I'll keep the civilians with me at Shandra Higheagle's ranch, thirty miles out Base Road. That's where you can send the team." Ryan turned to Shandra. "Do you have enough horses to haul everyone up here?"

She shook her head.

"They'll need to bring their own horses."

"This could take a few hours," the sheriff said. "It'll be close to dark. How far from the ranch is the site?"

"A good two hours by horseback." Ryan heard movement in the trees to the right. He stepped in front of Shandra.

Crazy Lil rode into the opening.

"Maybe we should wait until morning." The

sheriff's voice pulled Ryan's attention back to the phone. "It hasn't been found before now, I don't see what another twenty-four hours will matter. Go get a good night's sleep. I'll have the crew there at first light."

Ryan smiled. It looked like he'd be spending the night at Shandra's cabin.

Chapter Three

Shandra noticed Lil had herself pulled back together as they started back to the ranch. Not so uncharacteristic of the woman, she hadn't said a word. Didn't ask questions or even seem the least bit interested in the bones. Lil had her stubborn expression on her face. That meant there wouldn't be getting any information out of the woman until she decided to open up. Shandra had learned in the two years she'd owned the ranch and had Lil as an employee, not to press the woman for answers when she was looking stormy.

On the other hand, Shandra had lots of questions. The fancy boot meant he had to be someone of either affluence or high in cowboy circles whenever he, or she, though the boot was a large man's size, met their demise. Why was he riding on the mountain? Was he a hired hand for the previous owners who disappeared one day? If he was a hired hand, Lil should recognize the boots. She'd been on this ranch from the time her grandparents owned it until now. Though two of the owners since her grandparents sold the property had booted her off and told her not to set foot on the property, she'd just kept coming back like a stray cat. When Shandra bought the ranch and walked into the barn her first day of ownership, she hadn't been surprised to see the woman had set up residence in the tack room—bed, hot plate, and all—and was preparing stalls for Shandra's horses.

Not only had Shandra researched the land, she'd researched the previous owners and knew the history and Lil's connection. Believing the woman used the ranch as a shrine for her late parents and grandparents, and finding she was excellent with animals and a hard worker, she'd hired Lil. Knowing their boundaries with each other, they got along just fine. Shandra didn't pry into what Lil did when she wasn't tending the animals or helping in the studio, and Lil followed directions and helped with whatever Shandra asked.

Now, thinking about how this man could be connected to the ranch, she stared at Lil's back. Why had the woman taken off so abruptly at the sight of the burial? Had she recognized the boot and needed time to think about what she'd heard about a person's disappearance?

Scenarios and questions bombarded her mind.

When the path widened, Ryan rode up alongside of her. "Do you mind if I stay at your ranch for the night?"

His question was a vague muttering to the thoughts flying around in her head. She peered into his face. "What?"

The eager shine in his eyes dulled, and he sat straighter in his saddle. "Nothing. I just thought staying at the ranch rather than running all the way back to the station, to turn around and be here again at first light made sense."

She studied him as her mind moved from her thoughts to the present. "It does make sense. I wasn't questioning your motives. My mind was questioning who that person could be."

Relief eased the lines on his face. "That is if you have a guest bed."

Her mind quickly switched gears. "I'd love to have you as a house guest." They could barbeque and sit on the back patio and watch the wildlife while having a stimulating conversation. There was still a lot about Ryan he kept hidden. The couple of days he'd visited last month he'd learned more about her than she had about him.

"Why do you think Crazy Lil took off at the sight of the boot and bones?" Ryan asked.

Shandra smiled. "That's exactly what I was wondering. If the person I found was connected to the ranch in any way she would know them. She's been a part of this mountain and property since she was born. Her grandparents owned the ranch when Lil's parents died. She came here to live with them, and after the ranch was sold, she refused to leave. I've always thought she didn't want to leave because she had a deep connection to the property."

"Do you think Lil knows who you dug up?" Ryan's blank law-officer gaze landed on Lil's back.

"She could." Shandra watched Lil's body move as one with her horse and wondered if the woman had more secrets than why she refused to leave this land.

Ryan slid his gaze from Lil's back to Shandra's face. She was contemplating something. He'd heard rumors that Lil wasn't quite right in the head, but when he'd suggested to Shandra staying at her remote ranch with an unstable person might not be safe, she'd shrugged him off, saying Lil was as sane as she was.

When he'd met Shandra, she was a suspect in a murder, but he'd quickly ruled her out due to lack of evidence that she could have committed the crime. But Lil…the person had been dead a long time from the state of the decomposition. He shook his head. They didn't even know if there had been a crime committed. It could have been a hunter who became lost and died. But how did he get covered in clay? Ryan shook his head. No sense jumping to conclusions when they didn't have evidence to make a determination on the cause of death.

He relaxed in the saddle and enjoyed the scenery—nature and the woman next to him.

~*~

At the barn, Ryan helped Lil put the horses up while Shandra tended the clay she brought back.

"You have any idea who that person on the mountain could be?" he asked in a casual manner.

Lil's motions stalled a fraction of a second,

before she pulled the pack saddle off the horse Shandra had led down the mountain. "Can't say. There's been a lot of people get lost on that mountain. Could be a hunter, a hiker, a horseback rider."

"Ever heard of any ranch hands come up missing?" He continued unsaddling Shandra's horse. He set the saddle on the rack and turned back to Lil.

Her face appeared flushed, and her eyes glistened with tears. "No. I've never heard of ranch hands missing." She spun on her heel and led the two horses she'd untacked out to the corral.

Ryan gathered the lead ropes of the two he'd unsaddled and followed. Something was riling her up. He'd never witnessed the tough lady looking so shook up. *If I were a betting man, I'd bet on Lil knowing a whole lot more than she's telling.*

When the body is exhumed tomorrow and the state forensic lab has it, we'll learn the truth about who it is and what happened to him.

He released the horses into the corral and left the barn.

The studio door was open.

Ryan entered the area where Shandra made her fascinating vases that represented her heritage. He'd noted that while before her Nez Perce grandmother's death she'd made beautiful pieces, the ones she'd created since with more inspired details toward her heritage, had become even more remarkable.

She wasn't in the studio, but an open door

leading out the back of the building drew him.

He stepped out into the waning light of dusk.

Shandra had a trowel. With long strokes, she scooped clay from a bucket and spread it on four by four foot pieces of plywood.

"Why are you doing that?" he asked, leaning against the doorframe.

She looked up, pushed stray strands of her dark hair out of her face. "This is good clay but it needs to have the impurities taken out, so it will dry without cracking or breaking in the kiln." She scooped out of the last bucket that was standing up and spread it on the last board. "When this is dry, I'll break it up into powder and add water to make a slurry. After that has set for several weeks, I'll stir it and run it through a sieve. Then I'll leave it in the buckets until the water rises to the top and the clay is like mud." She stood, collected the buckets, and walked over to the water spigot on the side of the building.

"When the clay is like mud, I spread it on these boards until it stiffens, then I wedge it."

Ryan was in awe of the process it took for her to use the raw clay. "You cut it into wedges?"

Shandra chuckled.

The soft tone took his breath away. The more time he spent with the woman, the more he found himself attracted to her.

"No, wedging is what they call the process of folding and kneading the clay to make it workable." She placed the buckets upside down on a small rack against the back of the building and motioned for him to move into the studio.

"You go to a lot of work just to get the clay for your pieces." He couldn't hide the admiration in his voice.

She stopped and smiled. The sparkle in her eyes revealed he'd pleased her.

"Yes. Most potters purchase clay ready for them to mold into their creations. But I like knowing the clay comes from my land and Mother Nature's bosom. It gives each piece added life."

Her good humor vanished. A frown wrinkled her forehead. "I hope finding a body in my clay pocket doesn't taint the clay."

"I would think if the decaying body had tainted the clay, you would have noticed it by now." Ryan wanted to put the sparkle back in her eyes.

"The clay isn't fouled. It would have shown by now. It's the creativity. Knowing some poor soul was encased in the clay for who knows how long…." She shook her head. "I don't want my pieces to evoke sadness."

Understanding she put her feelings into each vase, Ryan put an arm around her shoulders. "I'm sure once the investigation starts and you realize the person died by accident, you'll be able to emote the same spirit into each piece as you have before."

"I hope so." She leaned her head on his shoulder for a moment. She heaved a sigh and stepped from his one-armed embrace. "How are you at barbequing?"

"Not too shabby." He fell in step beside her as they left the studio. His feet were light as feathers as he walked beside Shandra. They'd crossed a small but intimate moment when he put his arm around her and she placed her head on his shoulder.

He wasn't sure when or what the next step would be, but he was willing to go slow. The last woman he'd given his whole heart was marrying his brother in September.

Chapter Four

Shandra fed Ryan breakfast and had the horses saddled by the time trucks and horse trailers arrived at the ranch. She was surprised to see Maxwell Treat, the son of the local mortician.

"I would have thought the body would be brought to the funeral home," Shandra said, watching Maxwell lead a tall, large-bodied horse out of a trailer.

He smiled. "I'm not here from the funeral parlor. I'm part of the search and rescue group in this area, and I've helped dig up old bodies before."

"That's some horse you have there." Ryan said, slapping Maxwell on the shoulder.

Shandra had to agree. "What breed is…" She peeked under the horse which was easy to do it was so tall. "…he."

It would take a good-sized horse to haul Maxwell, a large muscular man, up the mountain.

"Zeus is part Clydesdale." Maxwell moved to help three other people Shandra hadn't met, as they loaded gear on their already saddled horses.

Ryan walked over to the other truck and trailer. People in county uniforms were preparing their horses.

Shandra glanced at the barn. She hadn't seen Lil all morning. When she'd peeked into the tack room, the area looked deserted. As if the woman hadn't slept in the bed or even made coffee this morning. Something was up. And it had all started with the discovery of the body yesterday.

She spun on her heel and headed to the barn for one last attempt to find Lil.

"We'll be leaving in ten minutes," Ryan called out.

Shandra waved her hand, continued to the barn, and stepped inside.

Silence.

She didn't even see Lewis, the cat that was Lil's shadow ever since the animal had arrived at the ranch. Not to arouse Ryan's suspicions, Shandra exited the back of the barn and strode into the back door of the studio. Lil also helped in the studio, cleaning up and loading the kiln. She wasn't here either.

"Her horse was in the corral, so she's not riding." Shandra had one last thought. Lil rarely set foot inside the house. Usually, only if she needed to make a phone call.

She exited the studio out the back and entered

the kitchen door.

Lil was on the phone.

"I know what you told me. But I have reason to believe he never left Huckleberry." She shook her head. "No, I don't need help. I'm not crazy. I'm numb!" She slammed the phone down and her shoulders shook.

"Lil?" Shandra stepped into the kitchen.

The woman jumped and spun around. Dark half-moons cradled her eyes. More lines etched her sixty-year-old face.

"What's wrong Lil?" Shandra moved closer. "You haven't slept."

"I'm fine." The woman started to walk by Shandra.

She put out an arm. "You haven't been right since you saw that boot. Do you know who that body is?"

Lil shook Shandra's hand off. "I don't want to go to the site with you. I have things I need to do here today."

"That's fine, but I bet if you talked to someone, you'd feel better."

"Shandra! We're ready to head out!" Ryan called.

"I have to go. I'll be back tonight if you want to talk."

Shandra hurried out the front door and over to Apple.

"Forget something?" Ryan asked, swinging up into the saddle on Duke's back.

"My lip balm." She wouldn't say anything to

Ryan about Lil's behavior until she'd had a chance to talk with the woman. Her gut said Lil knew something.

Sitting atop Apple, Shandra headed up the side of the mountain with a string of nine people following behind. By the end of the day, she hoped they would have the body dug up and possibly a clue to his, or her, identity.

~*~

Ryan was impressed with the skill and swiftness with which the team went to work. Shandra was allowed to help once she'd acknowledged she had uncovered what was showing so far and the expert said she knew what she was doing. The group knelt shoulder to shoulder slowly removing the clay and exposing more of the corpse.

Because he didn't have skills in excavating and was there to document the process, Ryan stood at the foot of the body, taking photos every time the group leaned back collectively to stretch their backs.

"I have something solid." Maxwell said. "And metal."

"That's the right area for a belt buckle," Alfred Harlow, a county deputy, said.

Everyone watched as Maxwell slowly uncovered what did turn out to be a tarnished silver belt buckle. He cradled the buckle in his hands as he stood.

"I've got stuff that will clean this right up."

"That's evidence and should be bagged." Ryan bent to pull an evidence bag out of his back pack.

Maxwell's long legs carried him away from the site. Not wanting to lose any evidence, Ryan followed Maxwell. "How long have you been a part of the posse? You should know not to tamper with evidence." Ryan stopped beside Maxwell.

"I started as a kid. They have a program that trains kids to help with searches. I got hooked but not enough to want to wear a badge every day." Maxwell tapped his rubber-gloved finger on the badge hanging on Ryan's belt.

"There's been days I wish I hadn't strapped on the badge." Ryan muttered, remembering the long weeks of rehab after being gunned down in a gang shoot out.

"What?" Maxwell's face and eyes left the buckle in his hands to stare at Ryan.

"Nothing." Just as curious to know the owner of the belt buckle and doubting it was a murder, he decided to let Maxwell have his moment of discovery. "How do you plan to clean that up?" Ryan changed the subject.

"I always carry toothpaste with me, it works great for cleaning up tarnished silver."

Ryan glanced over at the crew. They were all working diligently to get this corpse off the mountain today. It didn't matter the body had been here many years, the sooner it and the cause of death were identified they could close a case on a missing person.

Maxwell scrubbed at a section of the buckle with toothpaste and a toothbrush. Little by little the shiny silver was revealed. "This looks like a rodeo buckle."

The raised image of a cowboy on a bucking horse was taking shape as Maxwell rubbed off the dull-brown tarnish.

"Bareback Champion…Nineteen-seventy-four." Maxwell held the buckle up and stared at Ryan. "I think I know who this is."

"Who and how?" Ryan had been to a rodeo or two, but he wasn't up on any of the champions in the sport.

"I happen to dabble in the history of Huckleberry Mountain." Maxwell grinned and nodded.

"What does that have to do with rodeo?" Ryan wasn't too sure the man wasn't yanking his chain.

"Johnny Clark was ranked number one in the world in bareback riding in nineteen-seventy-four. Johnny Clark gave a couple of newspaper interviews in the early eighties here in Huckleberry. He was becoming a sought-after rodeo announcer. When he wasn't at a rodeo, he spent a considerable amount of time in Huckleberry. On this ranch." Maxwell frowned. "Rumor was he and the girl he was dating had an argument, and he walked out of Huckleberry in nineteen-eighty-four and no one ever heard of him again."

"I'm thinking this was a lover's spat gone wrong. But who would he have been dating—" Ryan knew exactly who he would have been dating thirty years ago. And who had made a hasty departure yesterday when she saw the boot.

Chapter Five

Shandra stood back as the law-enforcement team slid the skeletal remains onto a canvas tarp. She'd been stunned when Ryan told her Maxwell knew who the buckle belonged to and his assumed connection with the ranch. They wouldn't know that for sure until they arrived back at the ranch house and asked Lil if the remains were that of Johnny Clark and was she the girl he'd been arguing with before he disappeared.

Once the canvas was tied up in a long bundle the sound of a helicopter grew louder.

"Grab onto the horses!" Alfred hollered. Everyone but Ryan scrambled to grab their horses and moved out of the initial wind of the propeller. They didn't need to end up walking off the mountain if the horses spooked and ran away.

Shandra held onto Apple and Duke as Ryan hooked the bundled remains and clay they'd gathered from under the bones onto a rope. The tarp rose in the air and disappeared into the helicopter. Once the aircraft moved off, everyone started loading up their gear, getting ready to head back down the mountain.

"If it had been any later the helicopter would have had to wait until tomorrow morning to pick up the remains." Ryan retrieved his horse's reins from Shandra.

"I knew it would take time to dig the bones out, I just hadn't figured on it taking this long." She mounted her horse and reined him toward the path leading back to the ranch.

They moved single file down the path she and Lil had made the first month Shandra moved onto the ranch. Remembering the work they both put into making the path easy to navigate while leading a pack horse, she was pretty sure Lil had no idea there was a body hidden in the clay. She'd worked just as hard as Shandra to clear the way and had come up with better routes around barriers. Shandra could tell by the way Ryan had brought up the subject of who the body might be, he was already thinking of Lil as a suspect.

The best thing to do would be to get the whole bunch off her ranch as soon as possible, then sit down with Lil and a cup of tea and see what she could find out about Johnny Clark.

Shadows lengthened as they neared the last half hour of the trip. Horses became more skittish and tended to stumble more as they tried to pick up the pace, knowing they were nearing the end of the ride.

Shandra wanted to be at the head of the group when they came to the ranch to keep others from saying anything to Lil. Especially Ryan. She didn't need him going detective on the secretive woman. Lil would just lock her lips and toss the key down a toilet.

But how to get by everyone? There was a section of trail that widened enough for two horses to walk side by side, but it wasn't long enough to pass them all. She'd at least put herself ahead of Ryan, since the two of them were at the back of the line.

As soon as the trail widened, she squeezed Apple with her legs, urging the appaloosa to lengthen his stride and pass one rider, then another. By the time the trail narrowed again, she rode only three horses back from Alfred who took the lead off the mountain. Shandra twisted in her saddle to smile at Maxwell who had let her pass when there was barely enough room.

To her dismay, Ryan was right behind her.

Fiddlesticks! Now she wasn't going to be ahead of him at all when they reached the barn.

Fifteen minutes later the lights from the barn, studio, and front porch of the cabin welcomed them home. Everyone dismounted wearily and started preparing their horses to load in the trailers.

Shandra scanned the area looking for Lil. The woman didn't walk out of any of the buildings. She must be in her room in the barn. Indecision nibbled at Shandra. If Lil was in the barn, she didn't want Ryan finding her employee and questioning her.

"I'll take care of the horse. You probably need to catch up with the body." She reached out to gather Duke's reins in her hand.

Ryan moved the leather straps out of her reach. "Why did you move up the line back there?"

She stared at him in her best rendition of a college roommate who had used narcotics much too often to make her "feel artistic". "I was tired of bringing up the rear."

He narrowed his eyes. "That's a stupid reason to nearly run people off the path."

"I didn't run anyone off the path." She placed fisted hands on her hips. "Could it be you were the one who should have paid attention to where you were going? Or better yet stayed in the back?"

"Listen, you were the one who took off like a hornet was up your horse's ass."

She leaned back and stared at Ryan. Why was he so upset she'd hurried up the path? "If I had taken off at a gallop you could say that, but I moved Apple into a lengthened walk. There was nothing inappropriate about it." She pulled the reins from Ryan's hands. "I'll take care of my horses. Go do your job."

"I am. Where's Lil?" Ryan scanned the corrals, studio, and cabin.

"How should I know? I've been on the mountain all day same as you." Shandra pivoted and headed to the barn. She groaned inwardly when heavy footsteps along with the clomp of hooves followed her.

The minute she entered the barn her gaze landed on the crack under the tack room door. No light. Good. That meant Lil wasn't in her room.

Shandra tied the geldings to their respective stall doors and began loosening their cinches and unsaddling them.

She ignored Ryan who walked to the corrals behind the barn and back.

"You don't have any idea where Lil could be?" His tone said he didn't believe she hadn't a clue.

"Lil is a grown woman who comes and goes as she pleases. As long as she does her chores, I don't care what she does the rest of the time." Shandra lifted the saddle off her horse and packed it to the rack. She turned in time to catch Ryan lifting the saddle off Duke. He packed it over and placed it on the empty saddle rack.

"Why don't you gather more evidence? Just because you, Maxwell, and Alfred all think the skull looks like it was bashed in, doesn't mean forensics won't find an explanation." She shoved on his shoulder, spinning him toward the barn doors. "Go get more information then come back when you have it and question Lil."

He studied her over his shoulder. "You aren't trying to keep me from talking to her are you?"

Shandra hated lying. Especially to people she respected. "I am. I know Lil. If you go at her with all kinds of questions she could clam up, and you'll only get frustrated. Let me tell her what we found, and then see if I can learn anything that will help you. Break the ice for you."

"That's all you're trying to do, right? Break the ice, not obstruct justice." Ryan spun around, grasping her hand. "The last time you tried to prove a friend innocent you nearly got killed." He pushed stray strands of her hair off her face, sliding them behind her ear. "Let me do my job. It's safer for you that way."

She wanted to give in, let him take control of the situation, but her gut told her Lil was innocent. And though she had confidence in Ryan, he tended to think like a cop and sometimes, she'd learned, it took a little help from her ancestors to discover the truth.

"You can do your job. I'll be here for a friend if she wants to talk." She spun him again and pushed against his broad back. "Go get more evidence."

"I'll be back as soon as I have a coroner's report and irrefutable proof the corpse we found is Johnny Clark." Ryan stopped at the door. "In the meantime, stay out of trouble."

Before she could retort, he disappeared out the door.

Shandra let out a huge sigh. Relieved she no longer had to parry with Ryan, she started thinking ahead to how to reveal the information she knew to Lil.

Chapter Six

Ryan was still grumbling and shaking his head when he arrived at the Huckleberry Police Station an hour later. The corpse was flown directly to the State Police forensic lab in Coeur d'Alene, Idaho. If it had been a recently murdered victim, he would have hopped into the helicopter and escorted the body to the lab. He liked gathering as much evidence as quickly as possible. Considering after thirty years in the ground there was little evidence that could be contaminated, he'd wait for the report to be sent to him here.

Officer Blane, the overzealous young officer who had Shandra handcuffed the first time they met, sat at a desk smiling. "I hear you caught a cold case," he said.

"About thirty years cold. Is the chief in?" Ryan

had worked with the Huckleberry police force on several occasions. He liked the chief but didn't feel all the staff was competent.

"He's in." Blane went back to typing on a computer.

Ryan continued to the closed door with the placard: Chief Sandberg. He knocked twice.

"Come in."

He entered the room. The chief was of Nordic decent, with shoulders nearly as broad as his desk. His bushy blond eyebrows rose at the sight of Ryan standing inside the door.

"I understand you were called in for a buried body." Sandberg leaned back and motioned to a coffee pot on top of the file cabinet.

Ryan helped himself to a cup and sat in the antique wooden chair with arms. "Yes. Shandra Higheagle dug up a body in a pocket of clay on her ranch."

Sandberg leaned forward, placing his large arms on his desk and covering all his paperwork. "Why didn't she call us?"

"I guess she figured since it was out of the city limits it fell to the county, which it does." Ryan took a sip of coffee. He avoided wincing, having learned in Chicago you weren't deemed a real cop unless you could drink coffee that could rival battery acid. He turned the conversation to what he was interested in. "How long have you lived in this area, Chief?"

"Around twenty years. Why?"

"The skeleton had on fancy cowboy boots and a silver rodeo buckle. Treat thinks he knows who the man is. Some rodeo announcer who went missing thirty years ago. I wondered if you heard anything back then."

Sandberg shook his full head of light-blond hair. "Wasn't even near here thirty years ago. You might get a list of the locals living here at the time from Martha down at the recorder's office."

"Thanks, that's a good idea. Treat said he read about it in back issues of the paper. Turns out he's a history buff." Ryan downed the rest of his coffee. "In the morning, I'll ask Martha to start up a list, and I'll check out the papers."

"You need any help with leg work, take Blane. He's been itching to get out and do more detective stuff."

From the frown on the chief's broad forehead, Ryan had the feeling it was more a case of the chief needing his space from the rookie.

"If I get a lead, I'll send him to check it out."

Ryan stood, nodded to the chief, and exited the office and the building. He stood on the sidewalk contemplating the fact he couldn't do anything until morning.

A gnarling ball of fire sat in Ryan's stomach. I should have known better than to drink that strong coffee on an empty stomach. His gaze traveled down the street to Ruthie's Diner. The best place in town to get a home-cooked meal.

He had to eat and it looked like he might as well spend the night in Huckleberry. All the information he needed to dig up was here. He'd spent most of his nights the last time he was called in for a murder in Huckleberry in the back room of the police station. This time he'd get a room at one of the cheaper motels on the edge of town.

He stepped into the bright lights and country music of Ruthie's. He blinked and heard a familiar laugh.

Not unsurprisingly, Treat sat at the counter guarding a large plate of country-fried steak swimming in country gravy. Since Treat was engaged to Ruthie it made sense he'd be here enjoying her home cooking.

"Detective Greer, what brings you back to Huckleberry?" Ruthie asked.

"He was the officer in charge of the search and rescue I went on," Treat volunteered. "Detective, come on over and have a seat." Treat smacked the stool next to him. "You want to hear more about Johnny Clark?"

Ryan sat down and placed his ball cap on the stool next to him. "In a minute. I just had some of the chief's coffee. I need food in my belly." He glanced at the menu then pointed to Treat's plate. "I'll have what he's having."

"Good choice," Ruthie smiled, patted Treat's hand, and hustled into the kitchen. She not only owned the restaurant, she was the head cook.

"What else did you want to tell me about Johnny Clark?" Ryan took a sip of the water Ruthie had set in front of him when he sat.

"I mentioned to my dad that we might have found Johnny. He started in about how Johnny wasn't from around here but after his divorce had made Huckleberry his home when he wasn't following the circuit." Treat took a bite of his dinner.

Ryan mulled over what he'd heard. "So Johnny had an ex when he disappeared? Was it a bitter divorce?"

Treat shrugged. "Dad didn't say. I haven't had time to Google it and find out any more about them."

Ryan stared at the man. "Treat, this isn't a game. If it's determined Clark was murdered there could be a murderer whose felt safe all these years and wouldn't want to be discovered now. I'd sure hate for something to happen to you and have Ruthie on my back."

Ruthie walked up to the counter with Ryan's dinner. "Exactly. Maxwell, if you do any snooping into Detective Greer's investigation, you'll not be eating in this restaurant or warming my bed." She leveled her dark brown eyes on Treat and arched a black eyebrow.

"But Ruthie, you know how I like to research."

"No buts. Stay out of Detective Greer's way." She shifted her attention to Ryan. "If he so much as sounds like he's been sticking his nose in, you come tell me."

Ryan grinned. Ruthie wasn't a very big woman, but she knew the buttons to push on Treat to keep him in line. "I promise. I don't want him getting hurt any more than you do. It would look bad if I had to add him to my investigation since he was part of the recovery team."

He dug into his steak and potatoes while Ruthie

and Treat muttered quietly between themselves.

Several couples wandered in while Ryan finished his meal. He didn't know many of the people in Huckleberry, but he could tell by the way Ruthie greeted the customers if they were local or tourists. She knew all the locals and called them by name as she directed her waitress to seat them.

With his stomach full, Ryan was ready to settle in for the night. The night before he and Shandra had stayed up late talking and playing dominoes. She'd tried unsuccessfully to get him to talk about his life as a cop in Chicago. That was a part of his life he'd rather forget. Being part of a gang task force had put him in more danger than when he was in the military. And had landed him near death's door.

At the motel, he pulled out his laptop and Googled Johnny Clark, rodeo announcer. Just like Treat had said the man was divorced in 1980 and was ranked first in the world in bareback riding in 1974. What happened in the years in between? It appeared he married the year he rode so well. Then gradually moved lower and lower in the standings. Until he hit bottom with two arrests, one for drunk and disorderly and one assault. That was in 1980. After the last arrest, he divorced his wife and by 1982 traveled the rodeo circuit as an announcer. There was a photo of him at the national finals in 1983. Ryan stared at the photo. He couldn't swear to it, but the woman tucked against his side looked like a younger version of Crazy Lil wearing her signature purple.

Chapter Seven

After all the vehicles left, Shandra sat on the front porch waiting for Lil to return. By the time the drone of motors faded, the woman walked out of the woods.

"Lil, come have some tea with me," Shandra called to the woman before she ducked into the barn.

Her booted feet hesitated, then shuffled toward the porch. Lil's head was bent as she stared at the ground. She stopped at the porch steps.

"I'm feeling tired and would rather just go to bed," Lil said, not looking up.

"Lil, we need to talk. You know who that body is don't you?" Shandra wanted to reach out and make the woman tip her chin up so the brim of her hat didn't shade her face.

"I don't want to talk about it." She did a quick about-face.

"We have to talk about it. Ryan thinks you might have killed him." Shandra hated to blurt it out like that, but she had to make Lil see she needed to be prepared.

Lil spun back around. "I didn't kill Johnny! I thought he'd run off with someone else. We had an argument and he…he… accused me of things that weren't true and I slapped him." Lil grabbed Shandra's hands and squeezed so hard tears formed in Shandra's eyes.

"All these years I thought I was the cause of him not coming back. That he believed…" Lil dropped to the porch and hugged her knees to her chest. "I've been angry with him for thirty years. Now I know he didn't have a choice to come back."

Shandra dropped to her knees and hugged Lil.

"I don't understand what he was doing there, on the mountain," Lil mumbled. "There near the clay is the place we'd meet when Gran and Pappy said I was seeing too much of Johnny." She brushed the tears from her cheeks on the knees of her jeans. "Why would he be at our spot if he was angry with me?"

"Lil?" Shandra sat beside the distraught woman. "Lil, who would have wanted Johnny dead?"

"Dead? You mean like want to kill him?" Her fading blue eyes widened.

"Yes. It looked like someone hit him on the head."

"Oh no! Why? Why?" Lil rocked back and forth, tears streaming down her cheeks.

Shandra helped Lil to her feet. "Come on. Let

me get you to bed. You've had a lot of shock today. We'll talk more in the morning. We need to have some answers for Ryan when he comes back."

The strong-willed Lil allowed Shandra to lead her to the barn, into her room, and even take her boots off and settle her onto the bed.

Just before she switched the light off, Shandra noticed a wrinkled photo on the bedside table. It was a faded Polaroid of a tall, good-looking cowboy close to forty, and a young, thinner version of Lil. She wasn't wearing all purple like she did now. The only thing purple was a silk neckerchief tied around her neck. Lil glowed and smiled at the cowboy like he'd given her the world. This must be Johnny.

Shandra turned out the light, closed the door, and headed to her cabin. There was too much love and admiration shining in Lil's eyes in the photo and too much pain in the knowledge Johnny was dead for Lil to have killed the man. Tomorrow she'd ask Lil more questions and find someone from the man's past other than Lil to send Ryan investigating.

Sheba met her at the door.

"Where have you been? I could have used your company while I waited for Lil." She ruffled the shaggy black hair on Sheba's head and entered the cabin. A shower and good night's sleep was what she needed after being up late last night and the stress of today.

In the shower, she replayed the conversation between her and Ryan. Every time she asked him where he worked before he came back to Idaho, he changed the subject. Which she found odd when he'd already told her about his ex-girlfriend marrying his brother. That would be a pretty personal and emotional thing to tell someone. What could be worse than that?

She climbed into bed and shut her eyes.

Ella, her grandmother, hovered over the bed. Her smiling, wrinkled face made Shandra smile. Ella, it is good to have you in my dreams again. You have stayed away too long.

Ella cradled her arms and moved them in a back and forth motion as if rocking a child.

No, Ella, I am not ready for a child. I have to have a husband first. At the thought of a husband, Ryan's face appeared. Her heart sped and her mind traveled through all their good and bad times during their short friendship.

Slowly Ryan changed, evolved into Johnny Clark and she was Lil. They talked, hugged, and Lil backed away, spreading her hands over her stomach, an angelic smile on her face. Johnny's face became red and angry. Lil backed away, then turned and ran. The anger from the man scared and chilled her.

Shandra's body trembled and grew cold. She grasped the blankets to pull them snugger around her and woke.

Still trembling, she turned on the light. One o'clock in the morning. Sheba's body stretched across the bottom of the bed. "Sheba, I need your warmth and security."

The dog crawled up to lay beside her. Shandra stroked the large head. Why had Ella come to her now? And with dreams of Lil and Johnny?

She shook her head. Just because she gave you dreams that helped solve the last murder does not mean she is doing it this time. You only dreamed of Ella and Ryan because you are lonely. And you dreamed of Johnny and Lil because they are on your mind.

But what about Lil holding her belly as if she were pregnant?

Chapter Eight

The next morning Shandra boiled water, made tea, and added sweet rolls and fruit to the tray. She carried the tray out to the barn and used the toe of her boot to knock on the door of Lil's room.

There were stirring sounds coming from the other side before the door finally opened.

Shandra walked in, noting a box on the end of the bed with photos spilling out.

"I brought some breakfast and thought maybe we could talk about you and Johnny and see if we can find someone to send Ryan investigating other than you."

Lil was dressed in a large, purple and black plaid shirt over her usual nearly thread-bare jeans. Her white hair stuck out from her head like an explosion of stalactites. Without her cowboy hat, Lil looked like a woman wearing a spiked white helmet.

Watching the older woman, Shandra saw the resemblance to the young girl in the photo she'd seen last night.

"After you left last night, I lay in bed thinking about the last time I saw Johnny. We'd fought." Lil took a breath and continued. "I'd gone to see my mother's best friend. She'd become like a mother to me after Momma and Poppa died. Gran loved me and I loved her, but she didn't have the patience to listen to my problems or care that I'd fallen in love." Lil took the offered cup of tea. "She and Pappy liked Johnny well enough, but they didn't like that he traveled with the rodeo circuit and that I went with him on several occasions." She smiled wistfully. "Those trips with Johnny gave me some wonderful memories."

Her eyes glazed over and her expression relaxed, giving her face a younger glow.

Shandra took a sip of tea, allowing Lil to drift along on memories. When it appeared she was taking the long tour, Shandra cleared her throat and brought Lil back to the conversation.

"Why did you go see your mother's best friend?"

The question did the trick. Lil's eyes closed briefly then opened. Pain radiated from their hazy blue depths.

"I was shocked by Johnny's anger. He'd never gotten angry with me before. And his accusations… I didn't take them well."

"What did he accuse you of?" Shandra was

making mental notes. The fact Johnny had a temper was a sure sign he probably had someone somewhere he'd been in an altercation with.

Lil shook her head. "It doesn't matter now." She put the cup down and stood. "I've got chores to tend to."

Shandra caught the woman by her small wrist. "Lil, I can't help you if you don't tell me everything."

Lil peered into her eyes. "I've been living with the pain of Johnny deserting me for thirty years. Now that I know it wasn't on purpose, I don't want to dredge up any more pain." Lil pulled her arm free and walked out the door.

There had to be something more to this. Who was her mother's best friend? Maybe she'd be more willing to help keep Lil out of jail than Lil was.

Lewis, who'd been curled up on the pillow on Lil's bed, ran across the bed, bumping the box of photos onto the floor. The photos scattered across the wood floor as the cat flew out the door.

Shandra knelt and picked up the pictures closest to her. There was writing on the back. *Me and Johnny Cheyenne Days*. She turned the photo over and it was another photo of the two at a different rodeo. Again the only purple on Lil was the silk neckerchief tied around her neck.

Picking up the rest of the photos it was clear Lil had labeled all of them.

Shandra put the box on the table and started through the photos. She now had a visual of Lil's grandparents, an uncle, and there was even a photo of Lil's parents. Lil was a spitting image of her mother. Then she found a photo of Lil and a woman who looked old enough to be her mother. *Me and Momma's best friend, Sally Albright.*

She had what she wanted. The name of the woman who Lil had confided in all those years ago. *I hope she's still alive.* Shandra replaced the photos and put the box back on the bed. She collected her tray and headed to the house. She'd spend however long it took to find Sally Albright.

~*~

Ryan woke too early to catch breakfast at Ruthie's and too early to talk to any of the people he wanted to see this morning. He put on sweats and a T-shirt and went for a jog up the road out of town toward the ski lodge. This hour of the morning the traffic was light and the view spectacular. One of the reasons he moved back to Idaho was because he'd become homesick for the fresh air with a tang of pine, the majestic snow-covered mountains, and the lack of crime and violence. Six months after signing on with the Chicago P.D. he'd been ready to bail. But he'd signed a contract and he'd thought being in a big city would make Lissa see he could live in a big city.

He snorted. *Boy was I blind, not seeing she had fallen for Conor.* He'd dated a few women while in Chicago, but they all seemed fake. Coming back to Idaho he'd met a woman who wasn't fake. Just infuriating because she only saw the good in the people around her. How could Shandra side with a woman the whole community called Crazy Lil? There had to be a reason for them to tack crazy onto her name. Today he planned to learn all he could about the woman, the ranch, and the man they'd found.

His phone rang.

"Greer."

"That's short and to the point," Bridget, his little sister, said. "You must not have looked to see who was calling."

"You're right. Had I known it was you, I would have let it go to voicemail." He couldn't stop the grin when she huffed just like when they were kids and he'd aggravated her.

"Where are you? You're breathing heavy. I didn't catch you in the middle of anything….intimate?"

Anyone else would have been embarrassed, but his little sister was the only woman he knew that actually asked him for details when he dated. And not just what they ate. She asked questions that turned him red and caused him to stutter. He was pretty sure she did it on purpose.

"No. I'm running." He stopped and stretched his calves. "Why did you call?"

"Cathleen said you called in the other day from Shandra's phone. Are you two seeing each other?"

The innuendo in her voice wasn't lost on Ryan.

"No, we are not seeing each other the way you think. She found a dead body, called me, and I've been out there leading a search and rescue team to dig the body out. That's it." There was no way he'd tell her he'd spent the night at Shandra's even if it was in the spare bedroom. Bridget had a way of seeing things how she wanted to see them.

"I see. She called you. She should have called dispatch. Why do you think she called you?"

Ryan ran a hand over the muscles tightening in the back of his neck. Yep, his little sister was the only person who had ever given him a headache. In the military and in law enforcement, he'd never been frustrated to the point of pressure in his head.

"Bridge, I have to go. I need to finish this run and check on some leads. Why don't you call and harass the husband to be." He really wanted to get back to town, get breakfast, and start finding answers.

"You're dodging the obvious," she sang in that irritating voice she'd used when singing the k-i-s-s-i-n-g song as a kid.

"No, I'm dodging you and getting back to work. Bye." He pushed the off button and shoved the phone back in his pocket.

Shandra's face leapt into his mind. She was lucky. She didn't have siblings to call and harass her.

Did Lil have siblings? Or any family other than her grandparents? Something else to look into. Lil's family history.

He turned and headed back to Huckleberry. He wanted to be at the city recorder's office as soon as the door opened. The recorder could be putting the list together while he read through copies of the *Huckleberry Gazette* from 30 years ago and older.

Chapter Nine

"Why do you need a list of people living in Huckleberry from nineteen-eighty to eighty-four?" Martha Samples the city recorder asked.

"It's part of an investigation." Ryan tried to keep a smile on his face, but the moment he walked in and flashed his badge the woman had continued to ask questions.

"This have anything to do with the bones that artist at the old Whitmire Ranch found?" Martha licked the end of a pencil and jotted down the dates he'd mentioned.

"I'm not at liberty to say." Ryan started to back away from the counter. "Can you have that for me by noon?"

"Wouldn't surprise me at all if there were more than one body up there on that mountain."

Ryan stopped. "Why do you say that?"

"There's a reason Ralph and Virginia kept Lil on the ranch." The woman smiled smugly.

He was pretty good at reading people. The smugness was all show. He doubted the woman had anything factual to say, but he'd also learned sometimes what people made up could lead you to the truth.

"Why did they keep Lil on the ranch?"

"She was loose. Running off with rodeo cowboys and not coming home for days." She nodded. "They had to keep a tight rein on her."

He scanned the woman. She had to be close to Lil's age. "How do you know so much about Lil's grandparents when you appear to be about the age of Lil?"

The woman blushed. "I was three years behind Lil in school. Everyone in the school knew Lil liked cowboys. She followed the boys around who wore cowboy boots and word was any one of them could get whatever they wanted from her." She leaned closer. "If you know what I mean."

"That was in high school. In eighty-four she would have been about thirty. Was she still following cowboys around?" This was where he hoped to find a connection between Lil and Johnny.

"Oh, yes, that was when she was going off to rodeos with an announcer. He'd been a big-shot rodeo man. He had an accident. After that he took to announcing the rodeos. I can't remember his name, but he spent a lot of time in Huckleberry for about two years." She nodded up and down like a bauble head sitting on a car dash.

Ryan had some more things to discover. "I'll be back at noon for that list."

He made a right at the courthouse and headed to the newspaper office. The young girl at the desk showed him into a room with a microfiche projector and handed him several rolls of microfiche.

"That's nineteen-eighty to eighty-four copies of the gazette." She looked over her shoulder at the open door. "If you need help, just holler, I'll be at the desk."

He waved his hand as he slipped the film from the earliest dated box into the machine and listened to it whirl onto the reel.

Three hours later, he'd read accounts of Johnny, looked at several pictures of him alone and him with Lil. He read about a fire at the Whitmire ranch and how their son, Jerome, happened along in time to warn Ralph and Virginia, his parents, and save the barn. Conjecture was Lil had caused the fire, but the local authorities couldn't find enough evidence and the grandparents were adamant she didn't. But the girl refused to give an alibi. And Jerome held to the account he saw her slipping out the back of the barn moments before he saw the flames.

Ryan added Jerome Whitmire to the list of people to interrogate.

His phone buzzed. Glancing at the number, he quickly punched the on button. "Greer."

"I sent preliminary findings to Sheriff Oldham. He said you're in the field so here's the preliminary cause of death. Blunt force trauma," Sheila Rickman of the State Police forensic lab said.

"Could you tell what the cause was?" He knew

it would take a miracle for her to ascertain that information from a thirty year old pile of bones.

She laughed. "Oldham asked me the same thing. No. At this point all I can tell you is it was something heavy and round."

"Like a tire iron?" Premeditated murder would have the killer packing a tire iron to the site to whack Johnny in the head.

"No, the indention isn't that small. It's more the size of a driving club and swung with force. Here's the other news. I'm pretty sure it was the hit that killed him, but the way the ribs were cracked, he could have been knocked out and the force of the weight of the earth on him could have suffocated him before he came to from the hit on the head." She took a breath. "Or just over the years, the weight of the clay, that's the material we extracted from the bones, could have caused the deteriorating bones to crack. We'll know that better after more tests are run."

"You're calling the body a him. So it is a male?" Ryan had to get all his evidence clear and concise.

"Definitely a male."

"And you're definite it was murder and not a fall from a horse or something like that." His gut told him it was murder, but he had to cover all the angles.

"Yes, it was murder. The impact is too high on the head to have come from getting thrown from a horse. He would have had to land on the top of his head. As tall as he was that would have been impossible from a horse. From a cliff, it could happen."

Ryan jotted the information in his notebook. "We think we know who the victim is. I'll send medical and dental records to you today. Did you come across anything else you found odd?"

"Not odd. As would be usual the leather accessories, belt and boots, were intact, as well as the belt buckle someone had cleaned up before sending."

The tone of her voice made Ryan cringe. As a detective he shouldn't have let Treat clean the buckle up.

"Sorry about that. I had an overzealous rescue member."

"The dirt under the body that you sent produced snaps and buttons like on a western shirt and jeans. Also a key chain with the name Lil engraved. It had purple glass-cut beads around the edge. Not what a man would usually carry and I doubt the name was short for Lilburn."

"Purple and the name Lil." Ryan had enough evidence to question Lil Whitmire. "Thanks Sheila."

He hit the off button and stared at the screen. It was hard to picture the tiny woman in the photo gazing up at the cowboy could swing an object hard enough to kill him. But if she stunned him and shoved him in a hole…

Chapter Ten

Shandra stretched and picked up her phone. After an hour of fruitless searching, her next step was to call the city recorder's office and ask about information on Sally Albright. The phone rang twice and a pleasant voice answered.

"City Recorder's office, Martha Samples speaking."

"Ms. Samples—"

"Call me Martha, everyone does."

Shandra smiled. A friendly person, good. "Martha, I'm trying to find Sally Albright. Could you see if she still lives in Huckleberry?"

"Mrs. Albright does still live here, though her niece has been trying the last two years to get her to live at the new assisted living place over in Hafersville."

The wonder in the woman's voice intrigued Shandra.

"Why won't Mrs. Albright move?" Shandra needed the woman's address or phone number, but she'd play the gossip game to get Martha's alliance.

"She says she spent many wonderful years here in Huckleberry and all the people she loved are buried here." Martha's tone didn't approve.

"Well, I know as people age they become more obsessed with the past. I'm sure she wants to be buried next to her husband when the time comes." Shandra assumed the husband was dead since Martha hadn't mentioned the niece moving Mr. and Mrs. Albright.

"Yes, her first husband ran the local paper. Mrs. Albright was proud of the fact he allowed her to edit the newspaper stories. She taught high school English."

"Is there a chance you could give me either her phone number or her address? I have some questions I'd like to ask her." Shandra stared out the window watching Lil water the plants on the back patio. She needed to learn as much as she could about Lil as a young woman and discover why Ella was rocking a baby in the dream.

"I'm not supposed to give out that kind of information to just anyone."

If there had been authority in the way she said it, Shandra would have thanked her and hung up. But the undertone of the woman's voice led Shandra to believe she could get it.

"I really need to talk to Mrs. Albright about some people she knew years ago. I think they might be related to me, and I'm trying to discover more about them." It was a small fib. She did want to know about people Mrs. Albright knew, and Lil had become like family to her, so it wasn't that huge of a tale.

"Oh, who were they? Maybe I can help?" Martha's quick response proved she liked gossip.

"If Mrs. Albright can't help me, I'll come by the office and have a chat with you." Shandra wouldn't hang Lil's past out for the whole town to hear, but if she could make this woman think that she would, there was a strong chance she'd get what she was after.

"I'm sure if she knows the people, she'll be able to help you." The rustling of pages filtered through the phone. "You couldn't find her phone number because she is listed under her second husband's name. But she reverted back to her first husband's name after the second one was found dead after driving drunk and hitting a tree."

Shandra picked up a pen and tapped it quietly on the pad of paper on the table.

"Here it is. Five, five, five, seven, nine, six, three. When you see her, tell her I said hello."

"Thank you, Martha, I will." Shandra pushed the off button and stared at the number. This was her first clue to find out about Lil's past since the stubborn woman wasn't going to share. She dialed the number and listened to the phone ring.

"Hello?" The voice warbled a little and sounded like a pack-a-day smoker.

"Mrs. Albright?" Shandra asked.

"Yes. Who's calling?"

"I'm Shandra Higheagle. I own the Whitmire

ranch. I think Lil's in trouble and I need to ask you some questions about her past."

The woman wheezed. "What kind of trouble is Lil in? I promised her mother I'd look after her, but those grandparents didn't approve of me taking over as her mother."

"Could I come visit you? I don't want to talk about her problems over the phone."

"Yes. I haven't talked to Lil for a while. I don't know what kind of help I'd be."

"I need to know about her past. Specifically, Johnny Clark."

"That louse. Has he shown up after all these years?" The vehemence in the woman's words led Shandra to believe the woman thought Johnny had run out on Lil too.

"Yes, he has, and not in a good way. Please, would you give me directions to your place? I can be there in an hour."

Mrs. Albright rattled off her address. It was on the east side of Huckleberry. Shandra knew the location.

"Thank you. I'll see you in an hour."

She tossed a note pad in her purse and whistled for Sheba. She loved to ride in the Jeep.

Lil appeared out of the barn. "Where you headed to? I thought you wanted to work on those coasters today."

"I have an errand I need to run. I'll be back before dark. We'll work on the souvenir items tomorrow." Shandra climbed into the driver's seat of the Jeep and headed down the mountain. She'd just lied again. She hated it, but little white lies sometimes were needed to help people. And Lil needed help. She was Ryan's main suspect.

The drive to town rushed by as Shandra visualized the woman she was about to speak to. From the photo she'd seen in Lil's room she was expecting a well-aged woman who took pride in her looks.

Pulling up in front of a small rundown house with the fence in dire need of repair, that illusion flew out of her head. The type of woman she'd been envisioning wouldn't let the outside world see this decay of the place she lived.

"Sheba stay." She said, closing the door quickly before the dog squeezed between the front seats to leap out. The windows in the back seat were down half way to allow cross ventilation. She never locked her doors with Sheba riding. The huge dog was enough to deter anyone thinking of stealing something. While her bark was ferocious sounding, she would lick any thief to death and help him take whatever he wanted.

Shandra stepped through the gate hanging by one hinge and up the weed-gnarled sidewalk. At the porch she played hopscotch with the holes in the old boards and tapped on the door.

"Come in, the door's unlocked," called the voice she'd heard on the phone.

Shandra turned the knob expecting it to fall into her hand. But it stayed attached to the door and the door swung open. The inside of the house was neat and tidy. Various knick-knacks she was sure were collector items gleamed from cleaning.

A wizened replica of the women in the photo walked out of a room to the side of the living room. She pulled a small cart carrying an oxygen bottle and balanced a small tray with a teapot and cups.

Hurrying forward, Shandra relieved the woman of the tray. "Let me help. You didn't have to go to all this trouble for me."

"Honey, I figured if you wanted information on Lil and Johnny it was going to take a while and would parch my old throat." She motioned to the coffee table in front of a matching set of Louis the XV arm chairs.

Shandra set the tray down and took the chair opposite Sally. The woman parked the oxygen tank next to her chair and slowly sat. The clear tubing supplying Sally with her life-giving air was unobtrusive.

Sally leaned forward, extending her hand. "If you're a friend of Lil's I'm pleased to meet you."

"Shandra Higheagle." She took the old woman's small hand and squeezed slightly before releasing. "I am Lil's friend. She works on the ranch with me, and I've come to appreciate her uniqueness." Might as well dive in. "But it's her stubbornness about talking about the past that could land her in jail."

Sally inhaled deep then coughed. Once the coughing subsided, she peered at Shandra with watery eyes. "Jail? Why would that girl go to jail?"

"I bought the Whitmire ranch because it has two unique clay pockets that work well for my pottery."

The woman nodded. "I thought I knew that

name. The paper did a big write up on you when you moved here. And I saw some photos of your work at the recent art show."

Shandra smiled. "Yes, I wasn't a very willing subject for the article so they pretty much picked stuff up off the internet for the story in the paper."

Sally huffed. "They use the internet too much. Back when my husband had the paper, he went out and scrounged up the news, then he checked his resources to make sure it was the truth. Now-a-days they print whatever they want and call it poetic license."

"That's why I wanted to come to you for the truth about Johnny and Lil. Day before yesterday when I was digging in a pocket of clay, I dug up a cowboy boot attached to a body. I called in the authorities, and so far, no one has confirmed that it wasn't Johnny Clark."

Sally's eyes rounded. "Johnny? Did it just happen?"

"No. It looks like he was there for a long time. We're guessing thirty years."

"No…" Sally peered at something over Shandra's shoulder. "That means he couldn't come back, not that he didn't want to." She leaned forward. "How is Lil taking it?"

"Like Lil. She told me very little other than they had been lovers, quarreled, and he disappeared." Shandra poured two cups of tea and placed one in front of Sally. "Do you know what they were arguing about?"

Sally picked up the cup and sipped.

She was stalling. Shandra figured the woman's mind was spinning behind her lowered lashes as she dissected what she'd been told and decided what to tell.

Finally, after she'd sipped half the tea from the bone china cup, her eyes met Shandra's.

"This is Lil's story to tell, but you need to know to go easy with her. She has never gotten over Johnny's hurtful accusations and the feeling he abandoned them."

Shandra caught the last word. "Them?"

"Lil was pregnant. That's what they were fighting about. That's how Johnny got caught in his first marriage. The girl told him she was pregnant with his child. Turns out she'd been sleeping around and didn't know whose it was. After a quick wedding in Reno, a month later she lost the child. Rumor was she went to a clinic and had it removed fearing it wouldn't look like Johnny and he'd leave her. Only the regrets of taking a child's life left her an alcoholic, and Johnny's depression from his loveless marriage and an accident that shortened his rodeo career made him an alcoholic. He finally shook alcohol and was back on the circuit as an announcer when he and Lil fell in love. Only Lil's grandparents didn't like her being with a man ten years older who was divorced. They did everything they could to keep the two apart, which only made Lil more determined to be with the one person she felt loved her." Sally shook her head. "After her parents died and Lil went to live with her grandparents she shut down. Wasn't the fun-loving girl she'd been before. Johnny brought that back out in her. As much as I hate to admit it, he was good for her."

Sally drank the rest of her tea and nodded to the cup. Shandra refilled it and waited.

"The night those two had their fight, I was away at a teaching convention. Lil was sitting on my back porch crying when I came home. Her clothes were filthy and she had blood running down her legs." Sally's eyes saddened. "She'd lost the baby."

Shandra's heart ached for the reclusive woman who had suffered so much sorrow. Knowing how she took care of all the animals, she knew Lil would have been a terrific mother.

"She had no one to go to. The town talked about her enough, she didn't need them knowing the cowboy left her and she'd been pregnant. It's been our secret all these years."

Shandra reached across the table. Sally placed a hand in hers.

"It's our secret too. I can't imagine the pain that Lil has gone through all these years."

"Thank you. It means a lot to me that you'll be around to look after Lil." Sally's gaze roamed around the room. "She's the reason I haven't left this place. My niece has been after me to move closer to her in a retirement home, but I didn't want to leave Lil." She smiled. "I can now knowing she has a friend."

A lump formed in Shandra's throat. "I hope I can live up to the friendship you've given her."

Chapter Eleven

Ryan pulled up to Shandra's house. It was late afternoon and all was quiet. He didn't see her copper-colored Jeep. Sheba didn't bound around the side of the house. He stepped out of his SUV and walked up to the door.

He knocked.

No answer.

Scanning the area, he noticed lights on in the studio. She must be working. He really planned to talk with Lil but seeing Shandra was always a pleasure. And having her present when he questioned Lil might make the surly woman more cooperative.

The gravel drive crunched under his boots. At the studio door, he paused. Do I knock or walk in?

Thinking it was best to announce his arrival, he rapped on the door and opened it.

Lil stood beside a large round kiln, several square discs projected from between her fingers. "What are you doing here? Shandra went to town." She walked over to a work bench strewn with the small discs.

"I'm not here to see Shandra. I have some questions for you." He left the door open and leaned against the jamb, hoping to not look so official. The minute he'd said he had questions for her, Lil's invisible hackles stood on end.

"What kind of questions would you have for me? I don't know anything the police would be interested in." She walked back to the kiln and leaned into the large apparatus. Her head, arms and shoulders disappeared. A moment later, she straightened and had discs between her fingers again.

"Let's start with there has been a clear identification that the body Shandra found on the mountain is that of Johnny Clark." He studied Lil.

Her hands trembled a bit as she set the pieces down.

"I knew it was him." She ran the arm of her purple flannel shirt under her nose and shifted to walk back to the kiln.

He'd let her continue working if she kept talking. "How did you know it was Johnny?"

"By the boot. He wore those boots everywhere. He bought them after his first big pay check." She dove into the kiln.

"Someone could have stolen the boots."

She popped out with another load. "Nope. He only took them off to sleep, and then they were under his pillow."

Ryan cringed at the idea of sleeping on boots that had been through a rodeo arena. "Can you tell me the last time you saw Johnny?"

"Nope."

She had her back to him making it hard to read her expression.

"You don't remember the last time you saw Johnny?"

"I remember. I just don't want to." She spun back to the kiln and dove in.

Her reaction could be because she'd killed him.

"You can answer my questions here voluntarily or I can get a warrant and haul you in to the police station."

"Why would you get a warrant?"

The voice came from beside him. He'd concentrated so hard on Lil, he hadn't heard a vehicle approach. Turning his head, Ryan stared into the angry eyes of Shandra.

"Because she's being evasive with her answers and admits she doesn't want to remember the last time she saw him." Ryan crossed his arms. "I have proof she was with him right before he died."

"What proof?" Shandra crossed her arms and leaned against the other side of the doorway.

He shot a glance toward Lil who continued to unload the kiln. "A key chain with purple glass-cut beads and the name Lil was found with the remains."

Lil spun toward them. "He had my key chain?" She started mumbling. "That must be why he came back. But why to our spot?" She wandered to the window and stared out.

Shandra crossed the space between them and put an arm around the older woman's shoulders. "That's what we need to determine. What brought him back after your fight?" She glanced at Ryan. "Lil will admit she and Johnny had a fight, but he was alive when he stormed off." She narrowed her eyes. "You need to look elsewhere for a murderer."

Ryan didn't want to get on the wrong side of Shandra. He'd witnessed how ferocious she could be when defending a friend. Right now all clues led to Lil.

"I wish I could, but right now everything is pointing to Lil." Shifting his gaze to the older woman he asked, "Did you set fire to your grandparent's barn?"

"Why would I do that? There were always animals in the barn." Her wide incredulous gaze couldn't have been faked.

"You were brought in for questioning about that fire right after Johnny stopped coming around." Ryan flipped open his notebook.

"How do you know when Johnny stopped coming around?" Shandra asked.

"There was a write up in the paper that Johnny missed a rodeo job. A Phil Seeton stepped in."

Lil moved out of Shandra's arm. "That drunk only got the job because he was the only available person. He drank so much he wasn't on the first-hire list. He'd get in a fight with Johnny every time he saw him. Complaining he was taking away all of Phil's jobs. Once Johnny quit drinking he had rodeos coming to him to be their announcer."

"I'd think this is a better suspect than Lil." Shandra walked forward. "Lil had no reason to want harm to come to Johnny."

Lil's head spun so fast her ball cap sat askew on her gray hair. He didn't miss the questioning look on the woman's face.

"How do you know she didn't want Johnny harmed?" Ryan moved his gaze from one to the other.

"I've been talking to someone who stepped into Lil's life after her parents were killed. I can vouch that Lil had no reason to want Johnny dead." Shandra's gaze leveled on him. "That's as much as you'll get. You'll have to take my word for it."

Shandra wasn't about to spill Lil's pain out to Ryan. He'd have to take her word for the fact Lil had everything to lose with Johnny dead.

He shook his head. "You know I can't take your word. I have to find proof."

"Then go find this other rodeo announcer and ask him if he saw Johnny before the rodeo he missed." Shandra had been surprised to see Ryan's SUV parked in her driveway when she returned. But she shouldn't have been. He followed all his leads and from the sound of the key chain, he had ample reason to suspect Lil.

"You might want to talk to Johnny's ex, Tracy Gilley. She remarried and that husband came up missing several years after the marriage." Lil moved toward the kiln.

"Why would she have a beef with Johnny if they weren't married anymore?" Ryan walked over to the kiln.

Shandra had a pretty good idea it was so he could watch Lil for any telltale signs of lying.

"Every time we'd run into her on the circuit, she'd wail and hang on Johnny begging him to come back. The last time she looked at me and said, 'If I can't have him no one can.' There was an unnatural glint to her eyes. Johnny said forget it, she was just drunk." Lil walked to the bench with several coasters between her fingers.

Shandra bent into the kiln and grabbed more pieces. She placed them on the bench. Ryan's gaze was locked onto Lil.

"Any idea where I can find Johnny's ex?" Ryan asked.

"You can try looking her up through the barrel racers' registry. I think she still trains horses when she's sober." Lil returned to the kiln.

Shandra looped an arm through Ryan's and led him to the door. "You now have two people to investigate. Leave Lil and me alone so we can get our work done." She walked with Ryan to his SUV. "Do you really think that woman in there killed a man she loved?"

"Passion and personal betrayal are the number one reasons people kill one another." Ryan stopped at the driver's side door. "Most of the evidence I have points to Lil." Ryan placed a palm against Shandra's face. "Be careful."

She liked the feel of his hand and the concern in his eyes and voice, but she had nothing to fear.

"Lil didn't kill Johnny. She was shocked to know he was dead." She unlocked their linked elbows. "Thank you for your concern." She backed away. "Go catch the real murderer."

"I'll follow the new leads, but it's hard to consider it solid when the names were given to me by my chief suspect." Ryan opened the door and sat behind the steering wheel. "Call if you need anything."

"Don't worry about me. Ella came to me in my dreams last night. Lil isn't the murderer, but she does have secrets. Secrets the world doesn't need to know." She turned and headed back to the studio. The engine of Ryan's vehicle revved and the crunch of tires on gravel noted his departure.

Shandra approached the studio door with trepidation. She could tell by the way Lil watched her, she'd figured out who Shandra had visited with and that she knew Lil's deepest secret. Would the woman be upset Shandra knew all of her sorrow?

Chapter Twelve

Even with all the evidence against Lil,
Shandra's adamant denial she wasn't the murderer
stuck with Ryan. She'd been right before when her
grandmother came to her in her dreams and helped
her find the truth when her friend Naomi looked
like the suspect in the gallery murder. With that
knowledge and the way Shandra had leaned into his
hand when he placed it on her cheek, Ryan decided
to dig into Seeton and the ex.

He stopped at the Huckleberry Police Station.
The accusations Martha Samples made about Lil
were also eating at him. Had the crazy recluse really
been a loose girl back in the day? He didn't see it,
but felt inclined to do some research there as well.

Walking through the door, he spotted Hazel

Wells, a retired county worker who filled in as dispatcher at the Huckleberry Police Station. His sister, Cathleen, knew the woman and said she knew everything that had happened in Huckleberry from the time she could talk.

"Mrs. Wells, you're looking summery in that pink outfit." Ryan knew how to suck up to the older women. Comment on their clothing or their cooking.

"Thank you, detective. What is it you want?" Her eyes narrowed behind wire-rimmed glasses and her gray curls bobbed as she tilted her head slightly.

"I'd like to visit with you about some of Huckleberry's residents." He pulled up a chair, spun it, and sat with his legs straddling the seat and his arms across the back.

"This have anything to do with the bones you found on Ms. Higheagle's ranch?"

"Everything."

She picked up her coffee cup. "I'm due for a coffee break." Hazel was sprightly for her age and practically sprinted down the hall to the break room. Once inside, she filled her cup and poured one for Ryan.

"What or who do you want to know about?" She sat down at the table.

Ryan took the seat across from her. "How well do you know Lil Whitmire?" He might as well start with his first suspect.

"She was fun to be around until Junior High when her parents died in a car accident. She moved in with her grandparents and became quiet, kind of detached from everyone." Hazel took a sip of coffee. "She was younger than me."

"Was she loose? Liked the cowboys?" He asked.

"No! And what has this got to do with your bones?" She glared at him.

"Someone yesterday told me she was loose and followed every cowboy giving them what they wanted." He felt his cheeks heating relaying this information to a woman who could be his mother. Though he wouldn't blush saying it to his mother. His sisters had pretty much bomb proofed their mother of anything any of her children might say.

"Well, that person is lying. I don't think Lil so much as went out with anyone until Johnny Clark came to town. I'm not sure how they met, but once they did, you saw the two together all the time. Well, when Lil's grandparents didn't have her working." Hazel shook her head, making the curls bob once more. "Her grandparents acted like they were afraid they'd lose Lil like her parents."

"But they had other children…"

"Yes, Lil's dad was Virginia and Ralph's oldest boy. Then they had a girl who died of complications from pneumonia, and Jerome."

"Why didn't the ranch go to Jerome when his parents died?" Ryan pulled out his notebook.

"I think they needed money when they both started ailing and used the money from the sale of the ranch to pay for their care." Hazel stared at him from over the cup. "Do you think Lil killed Johnny?"

"She's my first suspect given her key chain was

found with the body and she admits to having an argument with him around the time he disappeared." Ryan took a sip of the coffee. It was better than the paint stripper the chief brewed in his office.

"Johnny was also seen arguing with another rodeo announcer." Hazel gave him a smug smile.

"How do you know this?"

"I was out with my husband at the Horseshoe bar in Hafersville."

"I thought Johnny wasn't drinking anymore at the time of his death."

"He wasn't, but the other guy was. He was so drunk he could barely walk to the door and as he was leaving he shouted he was going to get rid of Johnny Clark if it was the last thing he did. Something about losing work."

Ryan jotted her comment down. "But you didn't actually see the two together."

"Yes, we did. We stopped at a little diner on the way out of town. Johnny and this other guy were arguing. The other guy pushed Johnny. He shoved back and told him to get sober. Drinking was why he didn't have a job."

He circled Phil Seeton's name in his book. "Did you see either one leave?"

"Yes. Johnny got into his pickup and drove off. The other guy was cursing and carrying on. We went in and had something to eat. When we came out he was gone too." She tapped a finger on the top of his notepad. "Sybil at the style salon I go to in Hafersville mentioned that Johnny's ex had been in there when I was telling her about the argument.

She said that Tracy was going on about how she was going to get Johnny back or no one was going to have him. This was before her second marriage. One where that husband came up missing too."

"You're the second person to tell me that. Why hasn't anyone looked for the second husband?" Ryan jotted down a note to research Tracy Gilley's second husband. "You wouldn't happen to know his name?"

Hazel nodded. "Tucker Gilley. He was a pretty good roper in his day."

"So Tracy liked rodeo boys." He made a note of that and wondered if Martha hadn't been mixed up about Tracy and Lil. Which seemed odd for a woman who was in charge of records.

"She was a barrel racer back in the day before her drinking got in the way of her competing. Then she started training horses for barrel racing. I think she did pretty well."

"Thank you for the information. If you had to guess, who do you think killed Johnny?" He wasn't going to use Hazel's intuition to track down a murderer, but he thought it didn't hurt to see which way she was leaning.

"I'd say Tracy. She was known for her competitive nature. I could see her knocking off Johnny just to keep Lil from having him." Hazel stood, rinsed her cup and hung it on a peg above the coffee maker. "Looks like you're going to be busy following leads."

Ryan nodded.

Hazel left and Ryan pulled out his phone. He

dialed the county dispatch.

"Hey little brother, you still in Huckleberry?" Cathleen never answered his calls with the same decorum and business tone that she did with everyone else who called the Weippe Sheriff's office.

"Yes, I'll be here until I find the murderer of Johnny Clark. I need addresses for Tracy Gilley, ex-barrel racer and ex-wife to the victim, and Phil Seeton, I'm assuming retired rodeo announcer."

"Suspects?"

"Yes." Ryan flipped his notepad shut. "You can call me back with the information."

"Where will you be?" Her cryptic question wasn't lost on Ryan.

"At the Huckleberry Police Station. Where else?"

"I thought you might need a little R 'n' R with a certain woman by the name of Shandra. You invited her to Conor's wedding yet?"

He groaned inwardly. "No."

"Ryan O'Connell Greer, the woman needs time to find a dress. You better ask her soon or she'll say no just because it's short notice."

He didn't need a scolding from his older sister. "I'll get around to it. Right now isn't a good time to ask. She's not very happy I consider her hired hand a suspect."

Cathleen laughed. The sound lightened his thoughts and irritated. The same feelings he had thinking of Shandra's trust and faith in her employee.

"I have to go. Get me that info as quick as you

can. I need to get this solved." Ryan hung up on his sister and stared into the half a cup of coffee sitting on the table in front of him. Shandra knew something about Lil. Something that made her think the woman was innocent. If the woman had an alibi, you'd think she'd tell him.

He shoved out of the chair and decided to do his own digging into the rodeo circuit thirty years ago.

Chapter Thirteen

Shandra slopped more glaze onto the workbench. She'd returned to the studio after escorting Ryan to his vehicle and found Lil gone. Knowing the woman would return when she was ready, Shandra had begun the tedious process of painting glaze on the coasters she made for the local merchants to sell. They were squares of pottery with Huckleberry Mountain etched in them. It was a bit of added income for her and a way for the stores to have a memento to sell to tourists. Today was a good day for this process. Her mind wasn't thinking creatively. Her thoughts kept swirling to the two people Lil suggested wanted Johnny out of their way or dead.

An ex-wife saying she'd rather see Johnny dead than with another woman made a better reason to kill him than the rodeo announcer hoping to get his job. If other announcers had come up missing, then it would make sense that the Seeton guy had targeted the people who were keeping him from working. Targeting Johnny made no sense since there were other announcers out there to take the jobs. But to kill for jealousy and passion…that she could see from a woman.

She picked up the last fired coaster, slathered it with bluish glaze which would fire clear and shiny, and placed it in a tile rack to dry. With quick movements, she cleaned up the bench, dropped the brushes she'd used in the clean-up sink, and tightened the lid back on the jug of glaze.

Back in her house, Shandra went to the kitchen for a cold drink and then settled in front of her computer. Lil had said to check the barrel racers' registry. After an hour of putting in search words, she stumbled across a website for Tracy Gilley Barrel Horses. The woman had not aged well. No doubt from her years of alcohol consumption.

Her ranch was in southern Idaho. Shandra pulled up a map site and punched in her address and Tracy's. Six hours. She tapped her index finger on the edge of her laptop. Did she dare drive that far away when Lil could be hauled off at any moment?

She decided against meeting the woman face to face. But before she called Tracy Gilley, she needed to gather a bit more information about the missing second husband. She again did searches and discovered that Tucker Gilley had been a world champion roper and mysteriously disappeared while on a hunting trip with friends.

Shandra found the website for the newspaper where the Gilley's lived and entered the archives. She only had to go back ten years for the information. His wife Tracy was at a horse auction in Texas at the time of his disappearance. "Shoot. That makes it harder to find out if she was involved."

Clicking through the photos and articles about the man's disappearance she noticed a photo of a person she'd seen on Tracey's website. A man about twenty years younger than Tracy. She scanned the articles and discovered the man was a friend of Tucker. "Could he be the connection?"

Sheba woofed to come inside. Shandra walked to the kitchen door. Holding the door open for Sheba she spotted Lil entering the barn. She's avoiding me. Indecision weighed on her mind. Go see if she could open Lil to a conversation about Johnny and the child she lost or continue her digging into Tracy.

She'd give Lil some more space. Questioning her tomorrow might find her more agreeable. And she was in the middle of researching Tracy.

Her stomach grumbled. Six. Time had flown by. She placed crackers, cheese, deli turkey, and pickles on a plate and returned to her place on the sofa. Sheba padded in behind her, lying at her feet, with her head propped on the sofa cushions waiting for an offering.

~*~

Several hours later, her eyes burned and she was no closer to discovering anything. She did, however, know enough to call Tracy Gilley tomorrow and ask questions. Shandra closed her laptop, returned her empty plate to the kitchen, and poured a glass of wine. She returned to the sofa to watch the stars and relax before going to bed. Her eyelids grew heavier and heavier until she dropped into a blissful sleep.

Ella's face hovered in the sky as Shandra watched horses running in patterns in the field. Each one was a different color, leaving a glittering path in their wake. "Isn't this beautiful?" she asked Ella. Her grandmother shook her head. "You don't find beauty in the horses?" Shandra asked, puzzled. Her grandmother had loved horses and had taught her son how to speak with them. That was how he did so well at rodeos. Until that fateful day. Shandra's heart became sad. The horse's paths no longer glittered.

Ella nodded. Lil entered the dream. A gray cocoon of sadness wrapped her body. Shandra tried to get to her, to show her she cared, but a strong wind held her back. What does this mean Ella? I can't get to Lil, I can't ease her sadness. Why? What does this have to do with Johnny's death?

Barking woke Shandra. It wasn't a scared bark, but a happy bark. Shandra shook off the last of the dream and walked to the kitchen door where Sheba wagged her tail and peered out the window. Lil stood on the back porch in the glare of the motion-sensor light.

Shandra opened the door. "Come in. What are you doing out so late?"

Lil stood at the threshold her eyes downcast. "I

couldn't sleep thinking about what you did or didn't know." Her chin came up and her eyes peered into Shandra's. "I have to know what Sally told you."

Shandra smiled. "Come in. You have nothing to fear about what Sally told me. I can assure you, she only told me what I needed to know to help you." She grasped Lil's arm, pulling her into the house.

"Do you drink wine?" Shandra asked, releasing Lil and closing the door.

"Sometimes. Now seems like a good time to have a glass." Lil moved to the kitchen island.

Shandra plucked two wine glasses from her cupboard. She didn't want to chance Lil having a change of heart if she left the kitchen to retrieve her glass in by the sofa. White wine was always chilling in her refrigerator. She liked to wind down from her days with one glass.

"Here you go," Shandra placed a full glass in front of Lil and took the seat to Lil's left.

Lil sipped the wine for several minutes before she lifted her gaze to Shandra. "Did Sally tell you…"

"About losing the baby? Yes." Shandra kept her tone light. "She told me you and Johnny had a fight because he thought you were trying to snare him in a marriage like his first wife. And that afterwards, the same night, you lost the baby." She stared in Lil's eyes. "I'm sorry you had to go through all of that alone and carry it with you all these years."

Tears trickled down the gruff woman's cheeks. Gone was the tough cowgirl who said little and worked from sun up to sun down.

"I didn't get pregnant to snare Johnny. We used

protection. But when he started saying I must have been sleeping around and now was trying to put the kid on him…" She shook her head and bit her bottom lip. Her shoulders shook, but she didn't let the sobs Shandra saw in her body come out.

"He was just shocked. If you were using protection, his mind wasn't dealing with the statistics of pregnancies from failed protection back then. He only understood pregnant and feeling cornered. I'm sure the reason he was on the mountain in your meeting spot was because he'd realized his harsh words and had come back to apologize. " Shandra reached out, placing her hand on Lil's arm.

Lil's shoulders stilled. She tipped her blotchy, tear swollen face toward Shandra. "Is that why you think he came back?"

"I can't think of any other reason why he'd be in that spot on the mountain." Shandra took a sip of wine. "How did you two determine when you were meeting on the mountain?"

"If I wanted to see Johnny, I'd leave a note for him on the seat of his pickup and if he wanted to see me, he'd tuck a note in a hole in the corner of the barn."

Shandra sat up. "Did you look there after the argument, to see if he changed his mind?"

"I stayed with Sally for a week after I lost the baby. The day I returned to the ranch, there was a fire that started on that corner of the barn. The one Detective Greer mentioned I was questioned about." Lil peered into her eyes. "Do you think Johnny left me a note and whoever killed him set the fire?"

Shandra shook her head. "If the person knew about the note, all they had to do was collect the note and destroy it. There was no need to set fire to the barn."

Lil sipped the wine and sighed. "Are you going to tell the detective about the baby?"

Shandra sensed while it was relief to Lil that her employer knew the truth, she didn't want anyone else to know.

"I'll only say something if it's the only way to keep you out of jail. I wish Sally hadn't been gone that night. From what she said you were sitting on her back porch waiting for her. If she had been home she could say when exactly you showed up and hopefully clear you." Shandra tapped her fingernail against the wine glass as she spun the information she had around in her head.

"Marti Glasson saw me walking up to Sally's door. When I realized Sally wasn't there and Marti kept staring at me, I ducked around to the back of the house to wait." Lil took a swallow of wine. "Marti is the biggest gossip. She also had a thing for Johnny. She was jealous of the fact one night when Johnny and I were in the diner in Huckleberry and she was flirting with him, he ignored her and finally escorted me out of the place. He said he didn't like women who threw themselves at a man. He said desperation wasn't a turn-on."

"I saw photos of Johnny. He was a good-looking man. I imagine he had woman flocking around him all the time." Shandra hoped by directing the conversation to Johnny, she could learn more, and perhaps, pick up on maybe another person who might want him dead.

"Most of them kept their distance when he took me to the rodeos." She smiled. "He called me his little shield." Lil glanced up from where she'd been swirling her finger in the condensation on the wine glass. "When I told Sally that, she said he was only using me to keep the women away, that he didn't really care about me." She sighed and a soft, soppy smile graced Lil's lips. "But he told me he loved me, and that when he'd banked enough money to buy a ranch we'd get married." She wrinkled her nose. "I told him we'd have a ranch when Gram and Pappy passed. But he didn't want anyone saying he married me for the ranch."

The last statement struck Shandra like a lightning bolt. "The ranch was going to you? Why was it up for sale? And I thought you had an uncle who was still alive?"

"All my uncle ever cared about with the ranch was to sell it. He didn't have the same love of the land as my father and I had. That's why Pappy said it would go to me. But when their health started failing and they didn't have means to pay for doctors and such, I told them to sell the ranch. Even though they were stern and as Sally says, 'Tamped out my spirit', I loved them and they were all the family I had other than Uncle Jerome and his wife and stepdaughter. I haven't seen much of him since the ranch sold the first time. He and my aunt blamed me for talking them into selling."

"I would think he would want what was best

for his parents." Shandra was getting an unflattering view of Lil's uncle.

Lil shrugged. "He didn't come see them unless it was one of their birthdays, and he only lives thirty minutes away in Hafersville."

She thought back to Ryan's comment that it was Jerome who noticed the barn was on fire. "Was it one of your grandparent's birthdays the night the barn caught fire?"

Lil rubbed her temples and shook her head. "No. Everything happened so fast. I'd barely been home an hour when he came running in saying the barn was on fire. He and Pappy put it out and Pappy called it in as vandalism. After he and Uncle Jerome talked to the police, they whisked me to the police station and started asking me why I set fire to the barn." She took a sip of wine. "I just wanted to forget that night and everything that had happened after my fight with Johnny."

Shandra noted both their glasses were empty. "Why don't we go to sleep and tackle the puzzle of Johnny's death tomorrow?" She peered into Lil's eyes. "If we don't have secrets from one another we can work to find the person responsible for your unhappiness."

Lil nodded and stood. "I knew when you came and looked at the ranch that you were good for the land and the critters who lived here." She ducked her head and murmured, "Even me." Lil slipped out the back door before Shandra could think of something to say.

Chapter Fourteen

Ryan drove six hours to the ranch where Tracy Gilley trained barrel racing horses. From what he gathered on the internet, she did less training and more coaching these days. She was in her seventies, still thin and spry, but as his mother always said, her bones were getting brittle. If the woman took a fall from a horse it could be disaster.

The grounds were well-kept, the paddocks clean and tidy. A dozen horses of varying ages grazed in a large, white-fenced pasture. The woman had to be doing well considering the money it would take to keep everything looking this sharp.

He stopped his SUV in front of the walkway to the door of a large but not obnoxious house. The two white columns on either end of the porch didn't look out of place.

Ryan stepped out of his vehicle and scanned the area.

"Can I help you?"

A vaguely familiar man walked up from the barn. The closer he came, his image formed in Ryan's mind. He was the best friend of Tucker Gilley, Tracy's second husband. There had been many photos of him during the disappearance and then in the website photos of the ranch.

"Mr. Farley, I'm Detective Ryan Greer with the Weippe Sheriff's Department. I'd like to speak with Mrs. Gilley." Ryan held out his hand.

Farley didn't clasp his hand. He shoved his hands into his jean pockets and narrowed his eyes. "How do you know who I am?"

"Your photos were in the paper during the disappearance of Tucker Gilley and you're in the photos on the website for Mrs. Gilley's business." While he didn't have to tell the man, Ryan wanted Farley to know he'd done his homework.

The cowboy took a defiant stance, feet apart, arms crossed. "Mrs. Gilley isn't here."

"Where is she?"

"She's in Texas teaching a seminar on barrel racing." He continued to glare.

"When is she expected back?" He hadn't planned on the woman being gone. From all accounts on the internet she stayed home and worked the horses.

"Not till next week. What do you want with her?" Farley's hostility only made the man, and quite possibly the woman, look guilty.

"We found a body in Weippe County."

The man's face didn't lose its composer, but his tanned cheeks faded in color.

Ryan was pretty sure Farley hadn't killed Johnny Clark. He would have still been barely out of his teens. But where had Tracy's second husband gone missing? He searched his memory. That had occurred in another state. So why was the man looking like he saw a ghost?

"You know anything about an ex-rodeo cowboy named Johnny Clark?" Ryan pulled out his notepad to give him something to do and to look official.

The man stood straighter. "He was a damn fine bronc rider and did a good job announcing rodeos. He announced several I rode in. Why?"

"Did Mrs. Gilley ever mention him?" From what Ryan could tell Farley didn't know his employer had once been married to the deceased.

"No. But she would have been competing when Johnny was." Farley had uncrossed his arms now that the subject had drifted to rodeo.

"She was. She was also his ex-wife about the time he disappeared." He hid a smile as the man's jaw dropped and his feet started shifting.

"She was married to Johnny Clark? All be damned!" He shook his head. "She never mentioned that. Neither did Tucker." Farley grasped the front of his cowboy hat, lifted it, and scratched his head. "I do remember something about him disappearing from the rodeo circuit. Rumor was he'd married and settled down."

"He was murdered and has been buried on a mountain until three days ago." Ryan watched the man.

"Really? Dead?" Farley kept eye contact and didn't seem the least bit unnerved.

"Do you have a cell phone number for Mrs. Gilley? I need to contact her about the last time she might have talked with Johnny. I already made a six-hour trip for nothing." Cathleen hadn't been able to find a cell number for Tracy. And the house phone had been disconnected. That was why Ryan had made the long drive to talk with Mrs. Gilley.

"Give me your name and number, and I'll have her contact you when she returns." Farley was back to being protective of the woman.

Ryan pulled a business card out of his shirt pocket and handed it over. "Make sure she gets that and calls me as soon as she comes home. I need to get a time frame nailed down as to who was the last person to see Johnny before he was murdered."

Farley stuck the card in his back pants pocket. "Sure. Can't say for sure when she'll be back. She had planned to stay at a spa a few days before she came home."

"Which one?" Maybe he could contact her there.

"Echo Canyon."

"Thanks." Ryan jotted the name down in his notepad and closed it. "If I don't get in touch with her before she returns, I'd appreciate you giving her my card."

Farley nodded.

Ryan climbed back in his SUV and pointed his vehicle north. Next on his list was Phil Seeton.

~*~

As much as Shandra hated to ask any favors of her step-father, she was coming up against a wall when it came to finding out where Phil Seeton lived or anything about him. He'd had a lackluster career as a rodeo announcer and then just disappeared from the circuit as far as she could tell.

After a filling breakfast of waffles and fresh raspberries, she sat down at her desk and dialed the land line at the Montana ranch. If she was lucky he'd be out and she could have Mom ask Adam about Phil.

The phone rang four times and Mom's out-of-breath hello jogged her from her reveries of never feeling a part of Adam Malcolm's family.

"Mom, it's Shandra."

"Hello. You don't call near enough. How are things on your mountain?" Mom still talked with a whispery soft voice that made her sound fragile.

Shandra knew her mother was strong and tough as nails. Except when it came to her daughter. She'd allowed her second husband to take away all of Shandra's heritage from her biological father. Adam had insisted she use his last name even though he never legally adopted her. He wouldn't let her talk about her family at the reservation or tell anyone of her heritage.

"Not so good. I found a dead body in my clay pocket."

"You what? Found a dead body."

Mom said the words dead and body as if she had a bad taste in her mouth.

"Yes. It was Johnny Clark, a bronc rider from

the days when Daddy rodeoed." She knew that was a time that was never talked about. Another reason she'd been reluctant to call and ask Adam about a man who would have been part of the rodeo scene at the same time her father was riding the circuit.

"Johnny Clark? He was married to a barrel racer. Nasty woman. He was so nice, I could never figure that match out."

Mom was all about the social aspects of the rodeo, or so Shandra had gathered from what little her mother had talked about her days with the rodeo. She'd barrel raced a little before she'd caught Edward Higheagle's attention.

"You knew Johnny Clark?" Shandra asked, surprised Mom knew the man and was willing to talk about him.

"He was very nice, a good athlete until he started drinking." There was a pause. "Your father looked up to him," she whispered into the phone.

Shandra was shocked her mother spoke of her father. That she whispered was a sign she still wouldn't talk about him in the open. In the twenty-six years since Daddy died, talking about him had been taboo.

"Was he older than Daddy?" Shandra asked, willing Mom to keep the discussion open.

"Johnny was older, no longer riding, and one of the few who didn't give your father and I a bad time." Another pause. "You know. Our differences," she whispered.

"Is Adam there?" That was the only reason she could think of that Mom kept whispering when talking about her and Daddy.

"Yes, he is. Would you like to speak to him?" Her mother's tone became businesslike and her usual volume.

"Since he's still part of the PRCA, I thought he might be able to help me find another person who rodeoed with Daddy and Johnny. Phil Seeton."

Hissing like a tire losing air emitted from the phone. "Why would you want to speak to that lush?"

"He may have been the last person to see Johnny before he disappeared and ended up murdered." Shandra decided she wasn't going to tip-toe around the reason she was calling.

"You're not getting involved in another murder are you?"

The accusation in Mom's voice didn't deter Shandra from what she'd called about.

"My hired help is the suspect, and I know she's innocent. I'm just helping the local authorities find a new suspect." Which was true.

"I learned more about your last escapade in the local paper than I did from you. And it sounded like you were in danger. I don't like you sticking your nose in where it doesn't belong."

How many times growing up did I hear that? Usually when I brought up Daddy or asked questions about my Nez Perce family in Nespelem.

"Could I please speak with Adam?" Not that she really wanted to. She'd never been comfortable around the man, even as a child. As she grew up, she became even more uncertain of him.

"If you insist." The phone clunked onto the side

table in the living room.

Within a minute heavy footsteps approached.

"Shandra? Your mother said you wanted to speak with me."

Adam's gravelly voice and superior tone tossed her back to her teenage years. She'd been defiant. Especially the summer he'd planned a trip for him and Mom, preparing to leave her in the care of the housekeeper. She'd put her foot down and decided if they were going to leave her, she was going to a place where she was wanted—a place that would curdle Adam's and her mom's gizzards. She'd spent the summer with Ella.

"Adam. I was wondering if you knew the whereabouts of Phil Seeton. He rodeoed in the seventies and later tried his hand at announcing." There was no need for small talk. Neither one expected it of the other.

"Why are you looking up Phil?" The cautious tone made her smile.

What was he worried about?

"I dug up the body of Johnny Clark on my mountain. I'm trying to find a suspect other than my hired hand." This was true. She needed to find someone else for Ryan to latch onto besides Lil.

Adam whistled. "Did it happen when he disappeared, hell, about thirty years ago?"

"That's what the officials believe. I've had someone tell me that Phil had a beef with Johnny."

"I'll say. Johnny was getting calls from rodeos between the Pacific and the Mississippi to come announce for them. He did his homework and knew every cowboy that was entered into the rodeo and most of the rough stock." The awe in Adam's voice was something she hadn't heard before.

"That's what I've found too. And Phil was unhappy he couldn't get a job." She wanted to keep him on Phil. That was her goal at the moment.

"Phil was a raving alcoholic. No one could trust he'd show up on time and not be sloshed and sloppy." This was the stern and degrading step-father she remembered.

"Is there a way I can find him? I want to ask him questions about Johnny."

"I'll make some phone calls and let you know."

Pleasantly surprised he was willing to go to that much trouble, Shandra said, "Thank you, I'd appreciate it."

"I saw you're putting some Injun trinkets on your vases. It was bad enough you sign them with your Injun name and I have to explain that to your mother's friends but to add those trinkets and all, what are you thinking?"

This was the step-father she remembered.

"I'm giving tribute to my heritage and to my grandmother who left this earth without being allowed to give me the full benefit of her wisdom. Please let me know if you find Phil Seeton."

Shandra punched the off button on her phone and tossed it onto the couch. She walked out onto the back patio and breathed in the mountain air— untainted by bigotry.

Chapter Fifteen

Ryan's phone rang. He looked at the number and would have ignored the summons if he hadn't given Cathleen the task of finding information on Phil Seeton. He scooted to a sitting position in the motel bed and flicked his finger across the screen.

"What did you find?"

"It took you an awful long time to answer. Did I interrupt anything?"

Cathleen's cheery voice caused his body to shudder the same as when he heard shredding metal.

"Sleep. I had a long road trip yesterday, or did you conveniently forget?" Some days he wondered at his sanity for moving back near his family.

"I happen to have information for another trip. Not so long, though. Phil Seeton is residing in a low-income residential home in Missoula."

Ryan sat up and glanced at the clock on the bedside table. Seven. He could be there by ten even grabbing breakfast. "That's the best news I've had in a couple of days. Text me the address. And sorry for being so grumpy." He pressed the off button and dressed. He'd grab coffee and some pastries at Ruthie's and head to Missoula.

He didn't mind this drive so much. The Bitterroot Mountains were a spectacular sight no matter what time of year you travelled through them. Before dropping down into Missoula, Ryan pulled up the address and put it into the GPS on the SUV's dash. The facility appeared to be on the outskirts of town.

Twenty minutes later, he pulled into the visitor parking of the residence home and stared at a copper-colored Jeep Wrangler. He checked the license plate. Frustration and anticipation warred inside his chest. How did Shandra find Phil Seeton before he did?

Shandra sat in the chair opposite Phil Seeton. The old cowboy still wore boots and sported a large belt buckle. She wouldn't have been surprised if when he stood the weight of the buckle pulled his thin body straight over onto his long, pointed nose.

"Mr. Seeton, I'm Shandra Higheagle. I'm here to ask—"

"Higheagle? Any relation to old Edward? He was one hell of a bronc buster. I swear he talked to them horses before he got on. Half of them never bucked as hard when other cowboys rode them."

Shandra smiled. She might learn about Johnny Clark and her father this trip. "Edward was my father. Did you know him very well?"

The man stared at her for a long time. She was about to repeat her question when he raised a hand.

"You have his look about you. Not much of your mother." He set his hand back down on the arm of the chair. "You couldn't have been very old when he died."

"I was four." She swallowed the lump in her throat. Over the years her father's image had become the photos she pulled out every six months and studied. She couldn't remember him as well as she'd like.

"He was a good man. Damn fine man. Never could understand why people would put him down for bein' an Indian. Hell, Edward's family was here way before we were."

Shandra reached out to the man. "Thank you. You don't know how wonderful it is to find someone who doesn't condemn us for our heritage."

Tears came to the man's eyes. "Edward was a fine man. He told me if I left the liquor alone I'd beat him. But I couldn't climb on a horse's back without a little to steady my nerves."

Shandra felt a kinship with the old man. She'd finally found someone who knew her father and was willing to talk. "Did you travel on the same circuit as Daddy?"

Phil nodded his head. "Before he married your mom we traveled together several times." He shook his head. "I never did understand them. Fighting one minute and fallin' in the hay together the next."

He stared at her through rheumy eyes. "You were an accident. Edward insisted on marrying your mom when he discovered you were a bun in your mother's oven."

Shandra didn't know what to say. She'd never been told she was the cause of her parents' marriage. Nor did she know she'd been conceived out of wedlock. *Oh Ella, I wish you were here. I have so many unanswered questions.*

"That is a fact I didn't know about my existence." She smiled, when inside her mind was spinning.

Rapping on the door startled Shandra out of her musings.

The curly top of the attendant that delivered Shandra to the room appeared through the open door. "Mr. Seeton, you are a popular man today. You have another visitor."

The door opened wider, and Ryan stepped into the room.

"Shandra, what are you doing here?" Ryan asked, crossing the room and standing by her chair.

"Mr. Seeton and I are reminiscing about my father." This wasn't a lie. She'd yet to ask him about Johnny Clark and Lil.

"Mr. Seeton, I'm Detective Ryan Greer with the Weippe County Sheriff's Department. I'd like to ask you some questions about Johnny Clark." Ryan grabbed a hard-backed chair sitting beside a small table with a partially assembled puzzle. He placed the chair beside Shandra's.

"Why would the sheriff's department be

interested in Johnny after all these years?" Phil asked.

Shandra decided she'd let Ryan ask the questions unless he started making Lil out to be the villainess.

Ryan nodded toward her. "Shandra owns the old Whitmire ranch on Huckleberry Mountain. The other day while she was digging up clay, she dug up Johnny Clark's body."

Phil stared at Ryan, then her, then back to Ryan. "How long had he been there?"

"From all accounts, I'd say about thirty years." Ryan pulled out a notepad.

"Thirty years. That's a long time for no one to look for you." Phil rubbed a bony hand over his chin. "Now it makes sense that he missed that rodeo in Cheyenne. I couldn't believe when the rodeo committee called and asked me to fill in for Johnny. After he quit drinking he was punctual to a fault."

"I have a witness who saw you arguing with Johnny shortly before we believe he was killed." Ryan placed his pen on the notepad.

"Killed? You mean like murdered?" Phil stared at Shandra. "Now I know two people who were killed."

Shandra jumped onto his statement. "What do you mean?"

"What about you arguing with Johnny at the…" Ryan flipped through the pages on his book.

Shandra took the opportunity to capture Phil's attention. "What do you mean you know two people who were killed?"

"Horsehoe Bar in Hafersville. I have witnesses

to you threatening Johnny. And it had to do with rodeo announcing," Ryan said, ignoring her need to find out what Phil meant.

"That was probably a night when I'd had too much to drink and was blaming my problems on the nearest person." Phil waved his hands. "I did that a lot back in the day. I'd drink to get nerve to get up on the horse. A drink to numb the aches and pains from getting thrown off. A drink to celebrate staying on. A drink to feel bold enough to ask a cowgirl to keep a lonely cowboy company at night. I had a reason for every sip I took back then. Ironically, it was the rodeo that Johnny missed and I took over that I met a person who helped me get off the bottle and stay off."

"Do you remember where you went or what you did after your argument with Johnny?" Ryan persisted.

"Detective, I can't even remember if the time that's in my head is even the incident you're talkin' about. There are many days in my rodeo life that I honestly can't remember." Phil's eyes watered even more. "There are months of that life that I'd like to forget." He reached out a hand to Shandra.

She clasped his boney fingers in her hand.

"And there are others that I remember clear as day." He smiled. "Your father was one of the few who knew my drinking was a sickness. He covered for me and tried to make me see a better life without the bottle."

Shandra, again, was choked up knowing her father had been kind and helpful to another. "Thank you for calling him a friend."

Tears gathered in the corners of the old man's eyes. "He was a hell of a cowboy, and a hell of a man."

Ryan cleared his throat. "Mr. Seeton, did you ever meet a young woman called Lil who was Johnny's girlfriend at the time of his death?"

Phil released Shandra's hand, wiped at the tears with a blue bandanna he pulled from his pocket. "She was a likable gal. Always a smile. She and Johnny seemed to be the real thing. I was happy for Johnny. That wasp he married the first time stung him bad with her trailer hoppin' and drinking."

"Was there a falling out between Johnny and Lil?"

Shandra glared at Ryan. The man had pretty much said there was nothing bad happening between Lil and Johnny, why was he pressing so hard?

Chapter Sixteen

Ryan watched Shandra out of the corner of his eye. His main focus was on Seeton. The man appeared to be clueless about the disappearance of Johnny Clark. But the old man and Shandra had a connection. He was sure Shandra hadn't met the man before today, but in the time she'd arrived before him, she'd taken this man under her protective wing. It was clear by the way she kept glaring at him as he asked his questions.

"Mr. Seeton, you seem to have a fair amount of knowledge about Johnny, his ex-wife, and his girlfriend, Lil. Of the two women, which one do you think is capable of murder?" Ryan felt Shandra's gaze ease up on him.

"Johnny's first wife. She was a crazy bitch." The man reddened and looked apologetically at

Shandra. "Sorry about that. I shouldn't use language like that in front of a lady. My Sherry taught me that much in the years we were married."

"What about Lil? Did you ever see her and Johnny in an argument?" Ryan asked again. And once again, received Shandra's glare.

"I think I saw them arguing once. It was after his ex had words with Johnny. Lil looked angry. I seen Johnny talking with her. She pulled off that purple scarf Johnny gave her and stormed off, but it wasn't more than a little spat. They must have got over it because the next day Lil was wearing the scarf and smiling up at Johnny like he hung the stars in the sky just for her." Seeton smiled at Shandra. "That's the way my Sherry looked at me, and I couldn't keep drinking cuz I wanted to see that every day the rest of my life."

Shandra smiled. "That's what everyone wants in their life. A person that makes them see the good in themselves and loves them for the flaws." She patted the old man's hand.

At that moment, Ryan realized Shandra wanted a man in her life. Up until seeing her interaction with Seeton and her words, he'd been uncertain. She was a strong, independent woman, who rarely showed any vulnerability. This glimpse into her belief about a man and a woman, gave him courage to ask her to his brother's wedding. He'd do it as soon as they left this facility. He wasn't putting it off any longer. As Bridget said, the woman needed time to find a dress.

"So you feel Tracy Gilley had more motive to murder Johnny than Lil?" Ryan was seeing a pattern here. No one who knew Lil believed she could have killed Johnny. If Shandra's vehement denial hadn't been enough, all his investigating was beginning to make him a believer.

"I could see that woman killing anyone who didn't let her have her way." Seeton said nodding. "You know they never did find her second husband."

Ryan nodded. "Yes, but that isn't my jurisdiction. If she killed Johnny, I'll get her for that. I can't do anything about Tucker Gilley." Ryan stood. "Come on, Shandra."

She gazed up at him. Her golden eyes held uncertainty. "I'd like to stay a bit longer."

Ryan sat back down. "I'm seeing that you may be right about Lil. There isn't any more to learn here."

She shook her head. "Not about Johnny. Mr. Seeton knew my father."

The lost, wistful yearning in her eyes couldn't be ignored.

Ryan didn't care that the old man looked on. He grasped Shandra's hand. "I'll wait for you outside, there's something I need to ask you."

She nodded her head. He gave her hand a gentle squeeze and released it.

"Mr. Seeton, thank you for your cooperation." Ryan left the room and headed to the parking lot. He didn't feel like loitering in the hallway. There was something in Shandra's eyes. A vulnerability he'd not witnessed before that had his protective instincts kicking in. Something the man had to say about her father was going to upset her. He felt it in his gut.

~*~

When Ryan left, Shandra turned her attention to Mr. Seeton. "You said something earlier about knowing two men who had been killed. Did you mean Johnny and Tucker Gilley?"

The old man scratched at his chin again. "I guess that would make three, if they do find Tucker and he was murdered."

"Who do you believe is the third person you knew?" Her instincts and the drumming in her head already knew the answer.

"Girl, don't get yourself all worked up or into something that happened years ago. But there was no way your daddy should have been bucked off that horse." Phil shook his head. "He was one of the best at the time and that horse was one of the weakest buckers. He shouldn't have landed on the ground and that horse shouldn't have stomped all over him."

Nausea swirled in her stomach. No one had ever told her how Daddy died. Only that it was a rodeo accident. Her mind conjured up a mangled body smashed into the arena dirt.

"I'm sorry." Phil patted her hand. "I should have put it more delicate. I just figured you knew the whole story."

Shandra shook her head, willing the bile rising in her throat to stay down.

Phil handed her a glass of water. She gulped down half the glass and wiped at the tears slipping from the corners of her eyes.

"No one ever told me how it happened. They just said a rodeo accident. I never…I just…" She was at a loss for words. Ella had hinted several times that her son left the earth before his time. Shandra had thought it was a mother wishing her child hadn't been taken from her.

"Mr. Seeton, thank you for your kind words about Daddy and for this bit of information about his death. I never thought about looking into how it happened. I took my mother and step-father's explanation and didn't think about discovering the truth. Now that my grandmother is gone and my heritage was kept from me, I appreciate knowing the truth." Shandra gathered her fringed bag and stood. "I need to do some thinking about this after I make sure Lil isn't the one going to jail for Johnny's murder."

Phil smiled up at her. "I have a feeling you'll help Lil and find the real killer." He stood. "You're welcome to come back any time you want to visit about your father. He was a good man."

Shandra hugged the old cowboy. "I will definitely be back. Thank you."

Walking down the corridor to the main entrance Shandra played the conversation back over in her mind. "Daddy, knowing you had a painful end makes my heart ache."

Walking toward her Jeep in the parking lot, she spotted Ryan leaning against his SUV. He was a good-looking man. And caring. And he believed more in her grandmother entering her dreams than she did.

"What are you doing here?" she asked, leaning against her vehicle, facing him.

"Waiting for you. Remember, I said I'd be waiting, I had something to ask you." He remained leaning against his car, but the determined gleam in his eyes wasn't as aloof as the rest of him.

"What did you want to ask me? I hope it's not to butt out of this case because I can't. I found the body on my property and you are looking at my hired hand as the suspect." She scowled at him.

A smile curved his lips. It wasn't the first time her heart did a tiny thump at the sight of that smile.

"I told you my brother is getting married in September."

"To your ex-girlfriend. Yes." Her stomach started swirling but in a good way, not the way it had at Phil's news.

"My sisters are hounding me to bring a date and since you're the only woman I want to go to the wedding with… Would you be my date?" His gaze remained fixed on her face.

Shandra hadn't been on a real date in years. Once her steady boyfriend in college turned out to be a jerk and she'd been used by a professor, she had to be *very* interested in a guy to go out on a date. She was interested in Ryan. More than any man she'd ever come across.

"Yes, I'd be delighted to be your guest. Do I have to be nice to the bride? She did ditch you for your brother."

Ryan laughed. The deep timbre and crinkles at the corners of his eyes made her join in. "You may treat the bride however you see fit as long as you promise me all the dances."

Shandra held out her hand. "It's a deal."

Ryan grasped her hand and gently tugged her toward him. They stood toe to toe in the parking lot. The heat in his gaze and the possessive way his hand held hers, she had a feeling their first date would be the first of many.

"I think this deal should be sealed with a kiss."

His softly spoken comment stirred a whirlwind inside her chest. She swallowed and tipped her face up toward him. "Don't stick your tongue down my throat. This is a kiss to seal a deal not make out."

He chuckled. "I know you're the kind of woman a man takes his time unwrapping."

Before she could come up with a retort, his lips pressed against hers. The warmth and softness of his lips, the smell of his aftershave, and the glow warming her chest made this kiss a memorable one.

Ryan stepped back. "I have more leads to follow. I'll call you tonight."

Before she came down from the cloud of happiness the kiss had elevated her to, Ryan and his vehicle had left the parking lot.

She climbed into her Jeep, glanced in the rearview mirror at her reflection, and smiled. This kind of giddiness hadn't been in her life for a very long time.

Rummaging back through her childhood brought her to the truth Phil had told her about Daddy. "Once I get Lil cleared, I'm going to see what I can find out about Daddy's death. If someone caused it, they should be punished."

Chapter Seventeen

The return trip to Huckleberry was filled with calls to his sisters and mother to let them know Shandra would be his date for the wedding. All three women had screeched and nearly broke his ear drum. "Remember we haven't been dating long. Don't go making her think she's the next to get married. I don't want your enthusiasm to see me married scare her off." All three had agreed to be casual about meeting her. But he could already envision the excitement glinting in their eyes when they saw Shandra.

He pulled up to the Huckleberry Police Station in time to see Officer Blane run from the building and straight to the squad car.

Ryan rolled down his window. "What's up?" he called out.

Blane stopped, found who shouted at him, and grinned. "There's been a robbery at the Tasty Freeze."

"Go get 'em," Ryan said, stepping out of his vehicle. This was the perfect crime to keep Blane busy and out of the chief's hair.

In the building, Ryan took Blane's desk. He typed Echo Canyon Spa in the search area on the computer and found the establishment's phone number. Dialing the number he wondered if the guests were allowed outside calls. They'd have to make an exception. This was official business.

"Echo Spa and Resort, how may I help you?" asked a young, female voice on the other end of the call.

"This is Detective Ryan Greer of the Weippe County Sheriff's Office in Idaho. I need to speak with a client of yours. Mrs. Tracy Gilley."

"I'm sorry, our guests aren't allowed private calls." The young woman sounded apologetic.

"This isn't a private call, it's police business. If I can't talk with Mrs. Gilley then get me the manager of the resort." Ryan doodled on the corner of a paper as he waited. The soothing music coming from the phone while he waited only annoyed him. Fifteen minutes had passed when the music stopped.

"This is Grant Parrish, how may I help you?" The business tone was confident and cordial.

"I'm Detective Ryan Greer with the Weippe Sheriff's Department in Idaho. I'd like to speak with Mrs. Gilley about a body we found."

The intake of breath was the only sign the man

had been flustered before he explained why Mrs. Gilley couldn't be disturbed.

The man took a breath, and Ryan jumped in. "You don't understand. By not allowing Mrs. Gilley to speak with me you are obstructing justice."

"She came here to rest and relax. Since she's been here she's a changed person."

"That might be so, but I have a dead body that Mrs. Gilley was once married to. I need some answers." How many people did this woman pay to keep her away from the law?

"Married to? Did they finally discover Mr. Gilley? She'll want to know this."

Ryan wasn't going to say any different if it would get Tracy Gilley on the phone. "Now you see why it's urgent I speak with her."

"Yes. I'll check the schedule and see what treatment she's at. Hold one moment."

The music that was supposed to soothe, grated on his nerves some more.

The phone clicked, the music stopped, and a gravelly voice said, "This is Tracy Gilley."

"Mrs. Gilley, I'm a detective with the Weippe County Sheriff's Department—"

"Why are you calling me here at the spa?" The irritation in her voice made him smile.

"A body was discovered on Huckleberry Mountain. On the old Whitmire place—"

"Again, what does this have to do with…Whitmire? As in Lil Whitmire? Tell me it was her. That husband stealing skank had no right setting my husband against me."

"It wasn't Lil, and from what I've dug up so

far, you were his ex-wife when she came along." He'd see what she divulged before he told her who they'd dug up.

"He didn't really want to divorce me. All his rodeo buddies were against me. They didn't like him spending time with me instead of them."

"That's not what I heard. Rumor is you forced Johnny Clark to marry you by saying you were pregnant. Then once you had him hooked you either pretended to lose it or you visited a clinic."

"How dare you insinuate I'd be so cruel!" Her voice cracked.

Ryan was pretty sure he'd hit on the truth with the clinic. "The body we found is that of Johnny Clark."

"No!" she cried and began to sob in the phone.

"You're being pretty hysterical over an ex-husband when you haven't even blinked over the accusations you may have helped your second husband disappear."

"Why you! Who did you say you were? I'm going to speak to your superior and have you removed from the case. I'll not be insulted." Her bravado was back.

"Ma'am, you can't get me off the case, you're a suspect."

"A what? You think I killed Johnny?" She laughed. "If I was going to kill anyone it would have been that skank. I thought about it, when Marti told me she was pregnant."

"Marti who and who was pregnant?" Keeping up with the woman's conversation had him grasping at the details that stood out.

"Marti Glasson, she worked at the café in Huckleberry. She loved the cowboys. She also had a thing for Johnny. I knew he'd never fall for her. She had a roving eye and couldn't keep steady with anyone. But she and I had a mutual dislike for Lil Whitmire and when Marti told me Johnny had been in the café mumbling and trying to sort things out. She'd sat down to be his confidante and learned Lil had told Johnny she was pregnant. He was shocked."

The bulb in Ryan's head started flashing like the light on a squad car. That was what Shandra knew. But how did that make her so sure Lil hadn't killed Johnny when he refused to marry her?

"Did this Marti tell you what decision Johnny made?" His telling Lil he wouldn't marry her may have drove her over the edge. She would have met him on the mountain and smashed in his head. But she wasn't tall enough to hit him directly on top of his head.

"Marti called me back all hysterical a week later. She said Johnny came in with a ring. He'd decided to marry the skank." There was a nasty chuckle and, "Guess she didn't end up with Johnny either."

"Could that be because after learning all this, you followed Johnny up on the mountain and bashed his head in?" Just as Phil Seeton had said, Ryan could see the woman on the phone cold-bloodedly kill Johnny to keep Lil from having him. He saw no reason for Lil to kill Johnny. He was the father of her baby…what happened to the child?

"I did not kill Johnny! I wondered what happened to him but later I fell in love. True love with Tucker, and I hadn't given Johnny another thought."

Ryan stared down at the notes he'd jotted down. "Any idea where I can find Marti Glasson?"

"I doubt she made it out of Huckleberry. That one couldn't keep a job or a man for more than a week at a time." Tracy Gilley yawned as if bored. "I have another treatment in five minutes. If that's all detective, I'd like to get back."

"Yes, that's all. Thank you." While he didn't like the woman, what she said made sense and she'd given him another lead. Marti Glasson.

Shandra drove home on auto-pilot. She tried to keep her mind on Lil and how to prove she wasn't the murderer, but her mind circled to what Phil had said about Daddy. Then she relived the brief kiss with Ryan. This had been an eventful day.

Lil came out of the studio as Shandra pulled the Jeep into the garage. The woman met her at the door. "Did you learn anything from Phil?"

"He told Ryan he didn't think you could kill anyone, but he believed Tracy could." Shandra ruffled Sheba's ears and led Lil into the house. "Lil did you ever meet my dad, Edward Higheagle?"

"The bronc rider? He was your dad? I never put the two together." She smiled. "I met him once. I was with Johnny. Johnny liked to meet the competitors who were at the rodeos. We were walking around behind the chutes. Johnny was talking with the cowboys and getting some info to use when they came up. Johnny introduced me to Edward and told me to take a good look at the next world champion bareback rider." The happy reminiscing disappeared. "Your father was bucked off and died before he got that belt buckle."

"Were you at that rodeo? The one where he was hurt?" She had to know if Phil's declaration should be looked into.

"No, but when I heard I wondered if Johnny knew."

"I don't remember much about Daddy. Hearing Phil say nice things about him made me feel like I knew him better." Then her mind latched on to what Phil said about her being the reason Daddy and her mom married. As closed up as her mom had been all these years about the marriage, she doubted she'd get the truth from her.

"It's been an exhausting day. I think I'll make a salad and go to bed early. Tomorrow I need to check the clay I brought off the mountain and put it through the next phase."

"Do you think Phil said enough to keep your detective from badgering me?" A scowl wrinkled Lil's forehead.

"I think Ryan is starting to see you aren't the killer. But he has to keep digging to find who did take Johnny's life and ruined yours."

Lil walked over to her. "Thank you. No one has cared about me in so long, I forgot what it felt like." She wrapped her arms around Shandra and held on for several minutes.

Shandra returned the embrace, finding as much

comfort from the woman as she was giving. "You're welcome. I knew when I heard your background with this ranch you had to be part of it and my life."

Lil released her and backed away. "Thank you for allowing me to stay. It's the only home I know and,"—she ducked her head, then as if coming to a decision, peered straight into Shandra's eyes. "Our baby, mine and Johnny's, is buried on the mountain. That's where I go every Sunday. To be with it."

"I wondered why you disappeared. Now I'm even happier about my decision to let you stay." It was true. Happiness bubbled in her to know she had kept Lil on and that the woman could remain close to the only family she had.

"I'll see you tomorrow." Lil was back to her usual gruff, to-the-point attitude.

"Yes." Shandra couldn't stop the smile lifting the corners of her lips. Lil was a strong woman to have gone through all she had in her life. She was glad the woman was in her life.

After a quick dinner salad, Shandra took a shower and then sprawled across her bed, sketching an idea she had for a new vase and a surprise for Lil. Before long her eyelids grew heavy. She shoved the pad and pencil to the side of the bed and rested her head.

Lil stood beside the small waterfall on the upper reaches of the ranch property. She laughed and hugged a baby. Shandra stood by a tree watching the two and feeling happy. A gray cloud moved overhead. The air became cold. The wind picked up and Lil screamed. The wind tugged at the baby in the woman's arms. Shandra tried to help but the wind blew against her keeping her away. Lil clung desperately to the child, but inch by agonizing inch, the child was pried out of her arms. A woman's cackle startled Shandra. She looked everywhere but couldn't see who thought Lil losing her child was funny.

She looked up at the cloud, hoping the wind would blow it away. The fluffy contours of the cloud revealed Ella's face.

"What are you trying to tell me, Ella? Who would want to take away Lil's baby?"

Just then a tall cowboy came into view. He called to Lil. She spun toward him, surprise and then elation on her face.

A jazz tune burst into Shandra's dream, drawing her out of slumber and to the realization her phone was ringing.

Chapter Eighteen

Ryan was tired and should have just given in and closed his eyes, but he'd promised Shandra he'd call tonight. It wasn't that late. Ten. Surely an artist was up at this time of night.

"Hello?"

Her sleepy-sounding voice made him mentally slap himself. She'd made the same trip to Missoula he had today.

"It's Ryan. I told you I'd call. I didn't want you to think I was someone who promised and didn't follow through."

"Oh, what time is it? I dozed off."

"Ten. I can hang up if you'd rather go back to sleep." *Dunce! That sounds like an insecure teenager.*

"No, I was having a bad dream anyway. It's good to talk about something else."

The sound of rustling sent his mind to places it shouldn't go. Not yet anyway.

"Was your grandmother in the dream?" He found it ironic that he believed in the dreams Shandra had but she didn't. He'd learned her grandmother was an elder in the dreamer religion of the Nez Perce and had the ability to come to Shandra in her dreams and share knowledge she had about people. Usually the people she cared about that he was investigating for murder.

"Yes. But I don't want to talk about it." Her tone rang with stubbornness.

"Did she happen to tell you Lil had a baby?" He hadn't planned to launch that so soon but it seemed like the right time to bring it up.

"How did you know?"

The surprise and accusation in her voice made him smile.

"I investigate."

"Who else knows?" she whispered.

"Two others that I know of."

"Who? I thought only Lil, Sally Albright, and myself were all that knew about the baby Lil lost."

Shandra's accusing tone made him grin.

"Apparently when Lil told Johnny he wasn't happy about it."

"That's what they argued about before he disappeared. Johnny accused Lil of sleeping around because they used protection. Lil said she had only been with Johnny, but I guess that's how his first wife wrangled him into marriage was by faking a pregnancy." Shandra's voice shook with anger.

"When did Lil lose the baby?" Ryan had

latched onto that little morsel.

"That night. After Johnny left her on the mountain, she took off up the side of the mountain on a horse and fell off. Between the fall, the realization Johnny didn't want her or the baby, and who knows what else, she had a miscarriage that night. She showed up at Sally Albright's muddy, bleeding, and emotionally lost."

"That's something Marti and Tracy didn't know," Ryan said, more as a musing than a comment.

"Tracy and Marti knew? How? And are you talking about Marti Glasson? Lil mentioned her the other day." Shandra's questions came at him in rapid succession.

"Marti was working at the Huckleberry Café back then. Johnny came in muttering, 'she couldn't be.' The waitress discovered Lil was pregnant and Johnny wasn't happy. According to Tracy, Marti had a thing for Johnny, but she couldn't keep this juicy bit of news to herself and relayed it to the ex-wife." He still wasn't a hundred percent certain Tracy hadn't got even with Johnny.

"In my dream the baby blew away but Johnny came back. Did they happen to know if Johnny knew about the baby being lost?"

"From what I gathered they didn't even know Lil lost the baby. I'm pretty sure they figured she gave it up when Johnny left her." But, he hadn't asked that question.

"Do you know if this Marti Glasson still lives in Huckleberry?" Shandra asked.

"I happen to know she does. Only you know her as Martha Samples."

"I knew it!" The jubilation and affirmation in her voice startled Ryan.

"What did you know?"

"That that woman was a gossip and you could only believe half of what she said," Shandra said with conviction. "But she knew about the baby. Did she say anything else?"

"Johnny was in the café a week later with a ring. He'd decided to marry Lil." He listened close. Was that sniffling he heard? "Shandra? What's wrong? Why are you crying?"

"He came back to marry her." Shandra's words were wobbly.

"Yes…?" He'd never understand women. Even growing up with his two uncensored sisters, he still didn't know what they thought or felt ninety percent of the time.

"Don't you see? He did love her. He'd realized Lil would never try to trap him." The conviction behind her words grabbed his attention. "She said when they wanted to see one another, she'd leave a note in his pickup and he'd leave a note in the barn. They'd meet up on the mountain where his body was found. Someone found his note asking Lil to meet him. Someone who knew he was going to ask her to marry him."

"There are only two people. Tracy Gilley and Marti Glasson or should I say Martha Samples." Ryan was finally feeling like he had clear leads.

"When will you talk to them? I'd like to be there." She wasn't asking to come along, she was telling him she'd be there.

"I'm not sure having you there would be a good idea." He didn't need her butting into his interrogation. She might say something that would tick the other women off.

"What do you mean not a good idea? I'm a pretty good judge of character, and I might have some womanly insight to ask the right questions." Her voice purred.

He smiled and let the low husky words bathe over him. She was using her female wiles to try and sway him. She could try all she wanted, he didn't mind. But there was no way he'd have her in on the interrogations.

"Why don't you talk this way to me all the time?"

As expected she humphed and went back to business. "I could be an asset. Please let me be there."

"One of the interrogations I'll do by phone. Tracy Gilley is at a spa resort in Texas. I talked to her by phone today."

"This is the age of the speaker phone. I promise I won't say anything without your approval." Shandra didn't want to beg, but she would do just about anything to sit-in and hear the women's excuses for what they knew and if they had anything to do with Johnny's death. She owed it to Lil to find the truth. Once she heard for herself that Johnny had planned to marry Lil, she'd tell the woman. It was sure to lift a lot of the doubt that had veiled her life since his disappearance.

"Shandra, you know I believe in your instincts and your dreams. But I can't have you sitting in when I interrogate a suspect." The chuckle in Ryan's voice did little to soften his answer.

"We could just happen to be at Ruthie's the same time as Martha." She tapped a finger against the phone. "I happen to know she eats lunch there Tuesdays and Thursdays. Tomorrow is Thursday." She waited a beat. "And I'll be there whether you are or not."

"Listen, I can't have you investigating a witness without me." Gone was the mirth in his tone.

"Then I guess you'll just have to meet me for lunch at Ruthie's. Then we can call Tracy afterwards. I'm glad you're a man of your word. I'll see you at eleven-thirty at Ruthie's tomorrow." She hung up and laughed. It had been a long time since she laughed with a full heart. Johnny was going to marry Lil. They would have been such a happy couple. She could tell by the photos she'd seen of the pair.

"But I'll wait until I've heard what the other two have to say before I say anything to Lil. I want to have all the information in case she asks questions." She patted Sheba on the head.

Sheba opened one eye, watching her.

Shandra laughed again, and stood. Tomorrow could be the turning point in the investigation. She pulled back the covers and slipped into bed. There would be peaceful, happy dreams the rest of the night because her mind and heart were light.

Chapter Nineteen

The next day Shandra strolled into Ruthie's at eleven-thirty. She couldn't stay at the ranch with Lil and not say something, so she'd packed up vases to take to Dimension's Gallery owned by her friends Naomi and Ted. She'd spent two hours drinking tea and discussing art and the local galleries with the couple.

Ruthie greeted her when she stepped through the door.

"Shandra, welcome." Ruthie's smile was always genuine, lighting up her dark-brown eyes. Her mahogany skin glistened from working in the kitchen.

"Hi Ruthie. I'll have my usual lunch." Shandra took the corner booth that faced the rest of the café. This way she'd see Ryan and Martha enter.

Ryan appeared fifteen minutes later. He stepped through the door, removed his sunglasses, and scanned the establishment. There was a slight flicker in his eyes when he spotted her. Then his brow wrinkled in a frown.

She snickered to herself. He knew her well enough by now to know she'd be here.

After joking with Ruthie, he strolled over to Shandra's table.

Shandra couldn't take her gaze off the handsome detective. The memory of the kiss to seal their deal yesterday was still vivid. I wonder if we'll have a date or two before we go to his brother's wedding? I'm game.

"Hello Shandra, what a pleasant surprise," he said loud enough for the other customers to hear.

"Care to join me, detective?" she asked, smiling.

He slid into the bench seat across from her. His voice dropped to a whisper, "I wasn't surprised to see you here, but I'd hoped all morning you had come to your senses and were staying out of this."

"Not a chance." She smiled as Ruthie arrived with her usual cheeseburger and sweet potato fries.

"What can I get you, Detective?" Ruthie winked at Shandra as Ryan scanned the menu.

She didn't have a problem with the community knowing she and Ryan were a possible couple. She'd been celibate ever since moving to the mountain. She'd learned that the hard way--not all men are what they seem. That had taught her to be much more selective in who she became involved with.

Ryan looked up from the menu. Stared at her taking a bite out of her burger.

He nodded toward her. "Give me what she has,

but not those orange fries. I want real Idaho potatoes."

"You got it." Ruthie headed to the kitchen.

"That the sheep farmer in you coming out? 'Give me real Idaho potatoes.'" She joked, mimicking Ryan's voice.

"That's sheep rancher. And we grew a few acres of spuds. Yes, I like Idaho spuds," he replied and swiped one of her fries.

"Welcome, Martha. Your usual?" Ruthie called as the bell above the door tinkled.

"Hi Ruthie. Yes, the same as always." Martha laughed and joined another woman at a booth by the window.

"Any idea if the other lady will leave before Martha?" Ryan asked, stealing another fry.

"I didn't realize she met anyone. I just overheard Ruthie and Treat talking about Martha being a regular." Shandra bit into her sandwich and watched the two women.

Ruthie returned with Ryan's food.

"Ruthie, who is Martha eating with?" Ryan asked casually.

"That's Delia from the post office. The two meet on Thursdays. On Tuesdays Martha meets with Janine Whitmire."

"Whitmire? Any relation to Lil?" Shandra asked, wondering that she'd never heard of any other family members before.

"I believe it would be Lil's cousin," Ruthie replied. "Why?"

"Just curious. Lil never talks about family."

Shandra picked up a fry and pretended to be uninterested.

"Does Delia go back to work before Martha?" Ryan asked, taking a sip of his drink.

Ruthie's brow wrinkled. "What are you two up to? Do you think Martha has anything to do with that body you found?"

"Shh, Ruthie, we just want to ask her some questions without the other woman," Ryan said, quietly.

"Delia does leave first. Why don't you take her to the police station so my café doesn't get a reputation for being your headquarters?" Ruthie pivoted and returned to the kitchen.

"You know, she's right. You do a lot of your police work from this café," Shandra said, remembering the times they met here during the last murder they solved.

Ryan raised a dark eyebrow. "You invited me here. If you hadn't butted in, I would have called her down to the station."

"Oh, look. Delia's leaving." Shandra grabbed her purse and scooted to the end of the booth.

Ryan grabbed her hand, stopping her from standing. "Give the woman a chance to get out the door."

She waited until Delia was out the door and several strides down the block. "Now?"

Ryan released her arm and nodded.

Shandra picked up her iced tea and sauntered over to the booth where Martha sat pushing lettuce around on her plate.

"Mind if we sit down?" Shandra asked, not

waiting for a reply and sliding into the booth. She scooted clear against the window to allow Ryan space to sit beside her. No sense making Martha feel boxed in.

"I-I guess not. Ms. Higheagle, Detective Greer why would you want to sit with me?" Her gaze bounced from one then the other and back again. The fork pushing lettuce around dropped to the plate.

"I have a couple questions for you about Johnny Clark." Ryan pulled out his notepad, looking very official.

"I knew Johnny. Anyone living in Huckleberry in the eighties knew him. He was a regular visitor." Her gaze kept flickering back and forth between them.

Shandra wanted to ask questions, but she'd promised Ryan she'd let him do the talking. Unless, of course, he didn't ask something that needed to be asked.

"And you had a crush on him even though he was dating Lil Whitmire." Ryan stated the information like a news reporter.

"I don't know where you got this information. I can tell you there were many women, young and old, who thought Johnny was a catch. And to see him paying attention to Crazy Lil…well it made some folks wonder about his judgment."

Shandra couldn't let that go. "Why would anyone question his judgment for dating Lil?"

Martha leaned back and looked at Shandra like her face had cracked.

"Everyone knew Lil was inexperienced when it came to men. And Johnny, well he'd been married and had experience." Martha nodded her head as if agreeing with herself.

Ryan flipped through his notepad "But when I asked you why you thought the Whitmires kept Lil at the ranch, you said, "She was loose. Running off with rodeo cowboys and not coming home for days.' And now you say she was inexperienced. Why are you giving contradictory information in a murder investigation?"

Shandra couldn't stop the delight tickling her insides. Ryan had caught the woman in a lie. She studied Martha. Her cheeks had darkened, and her mouth was opening and shutting like a fish gasping for air.

"I, well I…"

"You've had a grudge against Lil for years because she caught Johnny." Shandra said. "Lil said you flirted with Johnny and he ignored you. That must have been a slight you couldn't handle."

"I was told you waited on Johnny the night Lil told him she was pregnant. Lil, the woman you despised, was going to have Johnny's baby. That irked didn't it? What I don't understand, is why did you tell Johnny's ex, Tracy?" Ryan flipped a few more pages on his notepad.

"According to her, you called to tell her the news. Were you hoping Tracy would do something to Lil?"

"No!" Martha stared at Ryan. "No. I just wanted to tell someone who could maybe persuade Johnny not to marry Lil. But then he came in about a week later, grinning and showing me the ring he planned to give to Lil. Said he was going to make Lil his wife." She groaned. "I tried to tell him she had been sleeping around, but he shook his head and said, 'My Lil wouldn't do that. Took me a couple days to realize she never had a chance to be with anyone else. When she wasn't with me, her grandparents had her up on the ranch.'" She sighed. "He was right. The only time she left the ranch was to be with him."

Shandra had a question. "Why didn't you say anything to Lil about Johnny going to marry her? All these years she's believed he left her because he didn't care. The one person in her life who loved her. You saw her at Sally Albright's the night she and Johnny argued. You could have told him he could find Lil there when he came back saying he wanted to marry her."

Martha dropped her gaze to the table. "I was hoping when he couldn't find Lil, he'd give up. I was hoping for another chance with him."

Shandra stared at the woman. "But you're married. Did you know Johnny was dead, so you moved on?"

"No! When he didn't come around after that night, I figured Lil turned him down and he went off and got lost in a bottle." Martha peered straight into Shandra's eyes.

The woman was shallow, but not the one who killed Johnny. Shandra glanced at Ryan. He was staring at Martha. No doubt, he was coming to the same conclusion.

"Who do you think wanted Johnny dead?" Ryan asked.

Martha shrugged. "The only one I ever heard threaten to kill him was Tracy. He got along with everyone else that I know of."

Shandra studied Ryan. He couldn't deny her listening in when he called Tracy. They were in this investigation together.

"Who else was in the café when Johnny came in flashing the ring and saying he was going to marry Lil?" Ryan asked.

Shandra smiled at Ryan. Someone else could have known Johnny was going to pop the question. *Good question.*

Martha stared at Ryan. "That was a long time ago."

"Who were some of the regulars? Take your time and think about it." Ryan coaxed.

"Mr. Ransford, he owned the Laundromat at the time. He's dead now. And Mrs. Albright. She'd just lost her first husband and would spend several nights a week in the café. Janine, I think. Yes, we were looking at the hideous bridesmaid dresses our friend picked out for us to wear at her wedding."

"Is that Janine Whitmire? Lil's cousin." Shandra asked to clarify.

"Yes. Only they didn't hang out together. After Lil's parents died, she didn't see any family but her grandparents." Martha shrugged.

"Do you know why?" Ryan asked.

"Not really. Janine's dad didn't do much with his parents. I think there was a falling out or something."

Shandra tucked this information away. "Anyone else?"

"There might have been. Once Johnny walked in, all my attention was on him."

Chapter Twenty

Ryan held the door to the café as Shandra exited.

"What I don't understand is if Sally Albright was in the café when Johnny came in with the ring, why didn't she tell Lil?" Shandra stopped in the middle of the sidewalk and stared at him.

"I haven't met the lady. Do you have an answer?" He enjoyed watching Shandra piece information together. It seemed to be as intrinsic to her as molding clay into art.

"I don't. But it appears to be the evening Lil went back to the ranch. Perhaps when Lil didn't become engaged Sally thought he'd changed his mind and didn't want to give Lil any more pain." She shook her head. "I'll have to visit Sally again and see what she says. You know, she wasn't very fond of Johnny. I wonder if after hearing Lil's side of things, Sally decided Johnny wasn't a worthy husband for Lil."

"That's all speculation." Ryan grasped Shandra's arm, escorting her down the street to her Jeep.

"Why are we headed to my Jeep? You need to call Tracy Gilley." She dug in her fancy cowboy boots, stopping her forward motion.

"I plan to call Mrs. Gilley." He crossed his arms. "You sitting in with Martha is all the sleuthing you're going to do with me today. Go find Sally and question her." Ryan pivoted and strode down the street. He didn't hear boot heels clacking down the street behind him, but he refused to glance back and see if Shandra got in her vehicle. He had work to do and the farther away from the woman he was the better.

When Ryan entered the Huckleberry Police Station, Hazel waved him over.

"Did my information about Marti being Martha help you any?" She pushed her glasses up her nose and bobbed her gray curls.

"Yes. It was the missing piece I needed to discover a liar. I'm still trying to find a murderer." He sat on the corner of her desk. "Did you think Martha killed Johnny?"

"No. That girl is all mouth and no brains. Are you still liking his ex for it?" The fading green eyes behind the glasses sparkled with interest.

"She's the best suspect I have at the moment. What can you tell me about the Whitmires in Hafersville?"

Hazel stood. "I think we both need a cup of coffee."

Ryan smiled and followed the woman down the hall to the break room.

Hazel poured two cups of coffee and placed them on the table. "Who in Jerome's family are you looking at now?"

When Hazel sat, Ryan took the seat across from her.

"I'm not sure. Martha said Janine was in the café the same night Johnny came in flashing a ring and saying he was going to ask Lil to marry him."

"Don't know where you're going with this, but Janine never liked cowboys. Rumor was she didn't even like men." Hazel took a sip of coffee and peered at him over the brim.

"She meets with Martha every Tuesday for lunch here in Huckleberry." An idea struck. "Was Janine swinging that way back in the eighties? Could she have been jealous of Martha drooling over Johnny and whacked him?"

Hazel spit out coffee and stared at him like he'd shouted profanities. "No! Janine wouldn't kill a man to get a woman." She reached across and smacked him on the forehead with a knuckle. "Knuckle brain, if a woman is drooling over a guy she wouldn't be interested in another woman. Janine knows Martha loves the men. They've just been friends for a long time." She shrugged. "And Martha doesn't care which way Janine swings."

"Shandra may be on to the killer. We discovered Sally Albright was in the café that night, and she had Lil's confidence, kind of like a surrogate mother." Ryan rubbed a hand across the back of his neck. *Maybe I should drive by this Albright's house and check things out.*

"Sally Albright is a nice, educated woman, but I've also witnessed her wrath. She and her first husband got in a public fight when he refused to publish some information she'd dug up that was damaging to a political figure. And then her second husband…they had many public fights. He was an alcoholic, and she wasn't about to put up with his drinking and being out all night. He died in an alcohol-related car accident. She's been single ever since. Back in the eighties she was between husbands and could have taken on the crusade for Lil." Hazel nodded and her curls bobbed.

"I think I better go check on Shandra. Excuse me." Ryan shoved the coffee cup to the middle of the table and hurried out of the police station.

~*~

"Mrs. Albright, sorry to bother you again but I have some more questions concerning Johnny Clark and Lil." Shandra stood on the front porch, precariously perched on the one board that looked new and less likely to give way under her weight.

"Come in. If you'd called ahead I could have had tea ready." Sally pulled her oxygen tank behind her leading the way to the Louis the XV chairs.

Shandra closed the door and took the vacant chair. "Detective Greer and I just finished talking with Martha about the night Johnny came in to the café with a ring and talking about marrying Lil. Do you remember that night? She said you were there."

Shandra placed her leather bag on her lap and fingered the fringe.

Sally drew in two long draughts of oxygen. "I was there that night. But I didn't know Johnny was crowing about marrying Lil. I think I left a few minutes after he arrived. That was the night Lil went back to the ranch. I didn't feel like eating at home alone so I went to the café for a little bit of company. This place felt lonely after having Lil stay with me for the week."

"I know it was a long time ago. Can you remember who was in the café?" Shandra stopped playing with the fringe and willed the woman to remember that far back.

"Well, there was Martha waiting tables, her friend Janine and another person in a booth. An older couple, I don't know who they were, Mr. Ransfield." She squeezed her eyes closed. "I don't remember anyone else. It was kind of quiet that night."

"Do you happen to know if Mr. Ransfield had any connection to the Whitmires or Johnny?" There had to be someone in that café that either followed Johnny or contacted someone who did.

"He was a widower that ran the laundromat. I don't think he had any connections with either." Sally put a hand on Shandra's arm. "How is Lil doing?"

"Knowing Johnny came back has helped. Now she knows he didn't abandon her. When I can tell her he was going to marry her that should help even more. But I don't understand who had a grievance with Johnny. It isn't making any sense." Unless

Ryan came up with more on Tracy, they were running out of people who wanted Johnny dead. At least the logical ones.

"Maybe it wasn't Johnny they wanted dead so much as to keep Lil from happiness."

Shandra stared at Sally. Her dreams. All of them showed Lil having her happiness taken from her. They should be looking for someone with a grudge against Lil.

"Do you know of anyone?" she asked Sally.

"Other than every woman who would have forsaken their marriages and boyfriends to be Johnny's girl, no."

Shandra shook her head. "This doesn't seem like a crime of jealousy. And if they wanted Johnny they wouldn't have killed him. They would have killed Lil." She stood. "I need to go have another talk with Lil. There has to be someone she has either forgotten about or is reluctant to talk about."

"Good luck. I hope you solve this for Lil's sake." Sally stood and started toward the door pulling her oxygen.

"I hope so too. Lil deserves closure and happiness." Shandra opened the door and was surprised to see Ryan's vehicle parked behind her Jeep.

She strolled to the driver's side door. "What are you doing following me?"

His cheeks took on a deeper hue. "I'm not following you. After talking to Hazel and her telling me about Sally's temper, I thought it would be a good idea to hang out and make sure you came out unscathed."

Her heart thumped. "That's sweet, but that little old woman can barely lift a fly swatter." She leaned on the window. "But between the two of us, we think we know who the murderer is."

Ryan's gaze traveled across her face, lighting a couple seconds on her lips before peering into her eyes.

"Who do you think the murderer is?" His voice dipped deeper, huskier.

"Someone who had a grudge against Lil. I don't think the murder was about hurting Johnny. I think he was killed to spoil Lil's happiness." She leaned in a little more and inhaled his spicy aftershave.

"This isn't the place or the time to be flirting with me." He slipped a strand of her hair behind her ear.

The statement, soft touch, and his fingers lingering near her cheek rushed heat to her cheeks and warm memories to her mind. She straightened remembering how those feelings had turned to horror once before.

When she focused on the man in the vehicle, she noted her pulling back had confused him. She smiled, drawing in a lung full of air. He hadn't hurt her all those years ago. She had to move forward and realize not all men were hurtful.

Ryan cleared his throat. "I'd like to take you out to dinner?"

"Why drive all the way to my place to pick me up, then come to town, then back, and return to town. That's four times you have to make the long drive. How about you just show up for dinner."

"I don't want you to have to cook." He protested.

"I enjoy cooking and it gives us more time to be together."

He grinned. "I like that idea." He started his SUV. "I still have to call Tracy."

Shandra was sure Tracy had nothing to do with Johnny's death. This was all about Lil. She needed to talk with her employee. "I hope you learn something helpful. I'm heading back to the ranch. I need to find out who Lil's enemies are."

"We can compare notes at dinner." His gaze held hers as she backed away from his SUV.

"I'd like that. See you about sixish?"

"If I'll be late, I'll call." Ryan started his vehicle.

"Perfect." Shandra strolled to her Jeep and climbed in. She didn't care if she had to ply Lil with wine, she was going to get some answers about her past and who would be cruel enough to want to ruin her happiness.

Chapter Twenty-one

Shandra stopped at the grocery store before leaving Huckleberry to make sure she had all the ingredients she needed for her special lasagna. It would be a meal she could prepare ahead of time, and they could visit while it baked.

At the ranch, Sheba greeted her and Lil came out of the barn. Shandra grabbed her bags of groceries. "Lil, I could use your help," she called.

The woman crossed the yard and picked up the last bag. "You feeding an army?" Lil commented, following Shandra into the house.

"Ryan is coming to dinner." She placed the bags on the granite counter.

"Business or pleasure?" Lil set her bag down beside the others and leaned against the counter.

"Pleasure." Shandra couldn't stop the smile that tugged at the corners of her lips. She'd contemplated her irrational behavior this afternoon and was determined to not let the past interfere with what could be a good future.

"You haven't dated anyone since moving here. You sure a cop is a good idea?"

Shandra glanced at the woman. "No. I know they have a dangerous job, but he's the first guy I can verbally spar with and not tick off, and he's the first that's made me feel giddy inside." She placed items on the counter as she talked.

"He's the one then."

The dull tone in Lil's voice caught Shandra's attention.

"The one what?"

"Your one true love. That's how I felt about Johnny all those years ago. That's why we slept together. I knew he was the one, and that we'd get married." The last word faded. Lil's eyes pooled unshed tears.

"I don't know if Ryan is my true love. We just started dating. But I know Johnny was yours. Lil, sit down. I have something to tell you." Shandra pulled out two chairs at the island. She took one, and Lil reluctantly sat on the other.

"While asking questions of people, I've discovered that Johnny was in Huckleberry the night you left Sally's and returned to the ranch. He was back to ask you to marry him."

Lil's despondent face became animated, then wary. "No. Who told you that?"

"Martha. She was working in the café the night you and Johnny argued. She knows about the baby."

Lil shook her head. "No, she couldn't. With her gossiping nature everyone in the county would have known."

"Well, she did tell someone. Tracy. As far as I can tell the information didn't go any farther than those two. I'm not sure why, but no one other than Sally, myself and now Ryan know about the pregnancy." Shandra hoped Ryan knowing didn't get Lil upset. But she seemed to ignore that fact.

"How did she find out?"

"After your argument, Johnny went to the café and was still mumbling and fuming. He told Martha. She was upset and called Tracy hoping she'd do something to you, I think. But I'm not positive. "

"Then why kill Johnny?"

The sorrow in Lil's eyes tore at Shandra's heart.

"I don't think they killed Johnny. He came into the café the night you came back to the ranch. Martha said he showed her the ring he was going to give you and ask you to marry him." She took a deep breath. "Lil, I don't think Johnny was the victim. He was the means to make your life miserable. Who do you know who would want to do that to you?"

Lil stared at her open-mouthed, her eyes blank under a furrowed brow. She finally found her voice. "I can't think of anyone who would be that cruel. Why kill poor Johnny? They could have spread rumors I'd been sleeping around and sent Johnny packing."

"That's what is bugging me. There wasn't a

need to kill him." Shandra slipped off the stool and grabbed two cans of ginger ale out of the fridge. She handed one to Lil. "Tell me about your cousin Janine."

"Janine? Not much to tell. After Momma and Poppa died, and I went to live with my grandparents, I didn't see much of my cousins or their folks. I never did know why Uncle Jerome was mad at Gran and Pappy. But since they didn't seem to care to fix whatever it was, I just went along with their wishes to not socialize with Uncle Jerome and his family."

Shandra thought on that a minute. "Then why did you call him when we discovered the body?" She took a sip of her drink and watched Lil. Uncertainty shadowed her eyes and wrinkled her face.

"I called to ask if he knew of any family that might have been buried on the mountain. He said no and asked why. When I told him you'd found a body, he started asking all kinds of questions. Ones no one had the answers to yet."

Shandra wondered why Lil's uncle had so many questions. She had some questions of her own she was going to have Ryan check out.

"I better get my lasagna made so I can visit with Ryan when he gets here." She slid the can Lil had barely sipped on toward her. "You can keep me company while I work. Tell me more about your life on this ranch. You've never told me as much as I'd like to know."

Shandra set out the ingredients she needed and

listened to Lil give the most animated history of the ranch she'd yet to hear.

~*~

Ryan hung up the phone at the Huckleberry Police Station. Tracy Gilley had admitted to all the things Martha had said and still remained adamant she had nothing to do with Johnny's death. He believed her. This was beginning to look more like a grudge against Lil, with poor Johnny as the fall guy.

He glanced at the clock on the wall. There was just enough time to take a shower at the motel and head to Shandra's. What kind of wine did she like? He knew the person to ask. The stop was on his way to his motel.

At the Dimensions Art Gallery, Ryan walked through the well-lit gallery, admiring the work by many local artists. Three of Shandra's newer vases, with the influences of her Nez Perce heritage, were on pedestals in the middle of the gallery. It was easy to see who the owners favored. That was why he came here to find out Shandra's favorite wine.

"Can I help…" Naomi Norton faltered when she recognized him. "Detective Greer, why are you here?"

He smiled inside. Even when he'd thought Naomi had killed the rival gallery owner, he couldn't make himself completely believe it. She was too straight forward.

"I'm not here as a detective. I know you are Shandra's closest friend and I want to know her favorite wine." Ryan glanced over at the nearest vase. "That vase is beautiful."

Naomi relaxed and smiled. "Her work has

become ethereal since her grandmother died. It's almost as if her ghostly spirit is helping Shandra create."

Ryan peered at Naomi. Did she know about Shandra's grandmother coming to her in her dreams? No, that was something Shandra would keep to herself. She wouldn't tell anyone until she believed in the dreams one hundred percent.

"Shandra invited me to dinner tonight. I want to take along a bottle of her favorite wine," he said, drawing the conversation back to the reason of his visit.

"Oh, sure! Wow, she invited you to dinner." Naomi smiled and her eyes sparkled. "I thought you two looked good together. That's what I told Ted."

"Thanks. We aren't a couple. Just getting to know one another." But he had plans to make it a life-time commitment when Shandra came around to the idea. Which led him back to wondering about her startled reaction this afternoon to his placing her hair behind her ear.

"Her favorite wine is any Riesling." Naomi winked. "Bring along a good quality dark chocolate and you'll score well."

"Thanks for the tip. Tell Ted, 'hi.'" Ryan left the gallery and headed straight for the wine and delicacies store. He picked up the wine and chocolate and headed to the motel. He was anxious to see Shandra's expression when he arrived with his gifts.

He didn't like Shandra finding dead bodies, but each time she did, it brought them closer together. If he didn't come up with some convincing evidence soon, the sheriff could pull him off the case. After thirty years and no leads surfacing, it was a waste of taxpayer's money to make this case his sole priority. Being pulled from the case would also pull him away from Huckleberry and Shandra.

Chapter Twenty-two

Shandra had everything made and the lasagna in the oven when the crunch of tires and Sheba barking floated through the open front door. Glancing at the clock, she smiled. He was ten minutes early. She might be an artist, but she believed in punctuality.

Sheba quieted. Eventually, boots clunked across the front porch. Shandra grinned. Ryan must have greeted Sheba with a full-belly scratch.

"Come back to the kitchen!" she called, placing the foil-wrapped French bread into the oven.

"It smells delicious in here," Ryan said, appearing in the kitchen door. He cradled a bottle of her favorite wine in one arm and held a box of her favorite chocolate in the other.

"How did you know?" She reached out as he

offered the two items to her.

"I am a detective, you know."

When she had a hold on the wine and chocolates, Ryan pulled them in next to his body, drawing her close.

"These are my thank you for a home-cooked meal and what I expect to be engaging conversation tonight. Your home-cooked meals this last week are the only ones I've had since the time I spent with you a month ago, but one of these days you have to let me take you out.."

It pleased her he enjoyed both her cooking and her conversations. Shandra cleared her throat. "I do make a pretty good lasagna, and I do like to converse about interesting topics. But I'd think with two sisters and family close by you would have attended a family dinner."

Ryan cringed and shrugged. "I've been invited nearly every week to a family meal, but I'm either working or not in the mood for my sister's badgering or my mother's less than subtle hints about her sons giving her more grandchildren."

Having been an only child with parents who were more than happy to have their daughter spend the night with girlfriends, she didn't understand his need to avoid his family but she understood the hints. It wasn't her mother and step-father who wanted her to marry and produce children it was her father's family. Her aunt and cousins hounded her when she attended Ella's funeral. Wanting to know when she would bring more Higheagles into the world.

"I'm looking forward to a great evening." Ryan

leaned across his offerings and kissed her lightly on the lips.

Shandra sprang back to the present and spun toward the oven. This relationship was going faster than any she'd ever been in. It needed to slow down. There were still many things about Ryan she didn't know.

A bottle clunked on the granite counter top.

"Would you like some wine now or with dinner?" Ryan asked.

"Now is fine. Glasses are in the cupboard right of the sink." She checked the lasagna, turned the bread, and closed the oven. A glass of wine sat on the counter in front of one of the stools. Ryan occupied the other.

Casually, she slid onto the stool and faced him. "How formal is your brother's wedding?" She sipped the wine and watched him. She wanted to know what had happened when he left Idaho that made him skip over those years, but she'd work her way to that topic later.

"I had assumed it would be huge with all the trimmings. Anyway, the Lissa I knew would have gone all out. But it seems my brother has tamed the social conscious beast in her. The wedding is going to be mostly family and outside. So don't wear tall spiky heels…" his voice trailed off as his gaze dropped to her legs covered in black leggings and on down to her bare feet.

His gaze returned to her face. "Actually you could wear this outfit. I like it." He took a sip of his wine. "A lot."

She'd never had a man like what her step-father called the "Bohemian" look. The tunic was bright colors and hit her mid-thigh. A wide belt cinched the sheath to her middle and the black leggings were comfortable. She hadn't dressed to catch Ryan's eye, only to be comfortable. It appeared he liked comfortable.

"I was going for comfortable." She sipped her wine.

"Comfortable, huh? I'd have guessed sexy."

While her insides leapt at his compliment, her mind shoved her heels into the ground. "Ryan, I invited you over to get to know you better before we go to your brother's wedding, and because I like you. But I'm not ready to make this a relationship." There I said it. Let him know where I stand.

"Giving a woman a compliment doesn't mean I plan to jump in the sack with her." Ryan's brow furrowed, and he leaned back in the chair.

She couldn't stop the hand that reached out, grasping his forearm. "I know. I'm just saying. It's been a long time since I dated and the last relationship I had…" She couldn't stop the painful memory from racing through her mind.

"I can tell by your hesitation and pain in your eyes wasn't a good one. What did he do to you?" Ryan's gaze searched her face.

"I'm not ready…" If she ever told anyone about her ordeal, it would be this man. But he'd want justice and there would never be justice for what she experienced. "I want to take things slow. Get to really know you so there aren't any surprises down the road."

His eyes narrowed. "Surprises. What kind of surprises?" He'd shifted to cop mode.

She shook her head. While she liked Ryan and felt more comfortable with him than any other man, she wasn't ready to divulge her past mistake.

"When I'm ready to discuss my past you'll know. Let's just enjoy tonight." She settled back on the chair and sipped her wine.

His gaze softened. "You mentioned a 'down the road' for us."

She nodded once. "I know you are the first in a long time to capture my attention. That means there is more to our connection than a one night stand."

Buzzing at the stove stopped the conversation. Shandra carried the lasagna to the table in the dining room. She'd set it earlier for the two of them. Back in the kitchen she grabbed the bread and salad.

Ryan picked up their glasses and the bottle of wine, following her into the dining area.

"This looks and smells wonderful." He set the glasses and bottle down and pulled out the chair at the head of the table.

"This place is for you," she protested.

"It's your house, your table, and your meal. You deserve the head of the table."

The sincerity in his eyes made her smile. She took the offered seat.

Once they were both seated, she waited a beat to see if he bowed his head to pray. She didn't give thanks for her food. She saved her discussions with God, and since her grandmother's death, the Creator, for meatier subjects. Such as world hunger and why he took her father at such a young age.

Ryan glanced at her.

She chuckled. "I guess I should ask. Would you like to pray before the meal?"

He shook his head. "I'm not a religious man. All the things I've seen in my life, it's hard to believe there's someone up there allowing so much hurting to happen in the world. But if you want to, I'll bow my head and give respect to your words."

"That's okay. God and the Creator know where I stand." She raised the spatula to dish up the lasagna.

"The Creator. So you also practice the religion of your heritage?" Ryan had learned a good deal about Shandra since their first meeting, but he'd come to the conclusion she didn't study her heritage.

"No, not really." She handed him bread, and then the salad. "Since Grandmother insisted I attend the Seven Drums Ceremony I've been studying the dreamer religion. It's fascinating and fits more to my ideals as a person."

He grinned. It sounded to him like she was practicing, or at least studying, the ways of her people.

"What was it Phil Seeton said to you that made you want to stick around the other day?" Ryan had noticed her reluctance to leave the man, and then an added reluctance to tell him what she'd learned.

"Just that he knew Daddy. I was so small when he died, I wanted to learn how others saw him." She avoided his gaze, but a smile lit up her eyes. "Everyone who knew him has wonderful things to say about him." She frowned. "Except my step-father. He forbid me to talk about Daddy, and when Mom would bring him up, Adam had nothing but bad to say."

"So your step-father knew your parents before the accident?" Ryan didn't know why this disturbed him. But it did.

"Yes. Daddy and Mom were on the rodeo circuit that Adam's family supplied the rough stock for. So they knew one another but really didn't run in the same circles." Shandra became contemplative.

Ryan didn't want to lose the mood of the evening. "I've ruled Tracy Gilley out as a suspect."

Shandra shook her head and took a sip of wine before settling back in her chair. "I think we need to look into Lil's family. She doesn't see why, but that's the only connection I can see that had knowledge of Johnny coming to the ranch. His murder had to have happened after he announced in the café he was marrying Lil. That's the last time anyone saw him."

"I'll pull everything we have access to tomorrow morning. Why would her own family want to ruin Lil's happiness? She'd already lost her parents." He knew so many blows to someone's stability and they'd start to crack. Was that what the murderer was after? Making Lil become Crazy Lil?

"Do you have any idea who started calling her Crazy Lil and why?" Ryan had a gut feeling if they found out who had tagged her as crazy they'd find the person responsible for killing the man who wanted to marry her.

"I first heard it from the realtor when she tried to chase Lil off the ranch. That was the first time I looked at the property. I never asked why people called her that." Her pretty face frowned. "I certainly have never called her crazy."

"I've noticed that." He liked that Shandra championed the underdog. He just wished the underdogs weren't always his prime suspects in murder cases.

Shandra stood and started gathering the dishes.

"Let me help. My mother made sure Conor and I know how to cook and clean dishes. She didn't want any woman we married to be stuck waiting on us hand and foot." He scooped up the lasagna and salad, following Shandra into the kitchen.

"It's good your mother was so forward thinking. I can't imagine a woman these days putting up with a husband who couldn't take care of himself or children." She placed the dishes in the sink and ran water over them. "You can rinse these while I put the food away."

Ryan smiled. Having bossy sisters it didn't bother him to be ordered around. Especially by a woman he respected. He sunk his hands into the water and piled the rinsed dishes in the second sink.

Shandra finished with the food and stood next to him, placing the dishes in the dishwasher. Working side by side, the silence didn't feel awkward. They worked well together. He bumped her arm with his elbow and grinned when she glanced at him.

"Don't get any ideas sheep herder." Her tone

was ominous, but her eyes lit with merriment.

Ryan burst out laughing. "You are not going to let me live down my childhood on a sheep ranch are you?"

"No. I grew up believing your wooly creatures were a threat to our livelihood. Though there were a lot of things my step-father told me that I've come to realize were untrue."

The one comment changed the atmosphere in the room as if a huge, dark, cloud hung from the ceiling.

Not wanting the cloud hanging over Shandra the rest of the evening, he decided to bring up a topic that would catch her interest.

"I went to the Dimensions Gallery to see Naomi and ask her about your favorite wine. They had three of your vases displayed in the middle of the gallery. The vases were exceptional in my opinion. Tell me about them." He led her back into the dining area, refilled their glasses, and escorted her to the back patio and porch swing.

Once they were settled, hip to hip, and shoulder to shoulder, sipping the wine, Shandra let out a huge sigh.

"Those three…I don't know how to explain it, but after Ella, Grandmother, died, I felt her presence." She stared down at her drink. "It was almost as if she took over my hands as I made each vase."

Ryan raised her face by cupping her chin. He stared into her eyes. "You had her on your mind. I would imagine her death filled you with regrets that you hadn't learned more from her. Did you ever ask her about your father?"

Her eyes filled with tears. "I tried to ask her. She said when I was old enough the truth would come to me." Her golden eyes, rimmed in tears, beseeched him. "I think the time is now."

Chapter Twenty-three

Shandra hadn't planned to draw Ryan into her belief her father's death wasn't an accident. It would take a lot of leg work and talking to many people to find the answer. But there was something about the man that made her tell him things she would normally never tell anyone, other than her trusty, silent companion Sheba.

His hand remained gentle on her chin. His thumb stroking back and forth along her jaw. But his eyes lost the softness they held moments before.

"What do you mean the time is now?"

"Phil Seeton said there was no way the horse Daddy was riding the night he died should have been able to unseat Daddy. I looked up the horse. He was known for stomping on the riders after they hit the ground." She leaned out of Ryan's hold on her chin and settled her legs up under her on the leather cushions. "Phil was pretty certain that Daddy didn't have an accident."

"Those are strong accusations and it happened what... thirty years ago?"

"Twenty-six, and this case you're working now is thirty years old." She sipped her wine. Now that she'd unleashed her thoughts into the open, she knew what she had to do. Prove or disprove her father's death was an accident.

"You'll have to do a lot of digging. What does your mother say about the accident?"

Ryan sipped his wine, but his intent gaze told her he was back in cop mode.

"She never talks about it. They, Mom and Adam, told me it was an accident, that's it. I never thought to see what kind of accident. It was Phil who told me about Daddy falling off and the horse stomping him…" She couldn't say more. Each time the image formed in her mind, bile rose in her throat.

"You need answers. That's clear by how emotional you get talking about your father's death." Ryan set his wine glass down and grasped her shoulders, turning her to face him. "Do some digging, but if you get even an inkling about someone or find proof it wasn't an accident, promise you'll tell me. I don't want something happening to you."

She'd never had a man stare at her with such possessiveness or concern. Up until meeting Ryan, she'd sworn off getting close to a man. Now staring into this man's eyes, she could feel his honest concern and see a lifetime with him.

"I promise to keep you abreast of whatever I find. I don't think I could do this if I didn't have you to help me interpret what I find."

His gaze heated, and he drew her against his chest. Their lips met. Her heart thrummed and she returned the kiss.

When her body started to melt under his hands and her mind started to haze, she pushed lightly against his body, putting space between them. She needed time to process the emotions and his reactions.

Ryan released her, leaning back on the porch swing watching her. "Too fast?"

"Yes. No. I don't know. I told you it's been a while since I was in a relationship." *And it turned ugly*. She picked up her wine as a way to avoid eye contact.

"I haven't been serious about anyone since Lissa."

He said it casually, but she understood. His heart had been broken, and he'd kept it to himself. That he was confiding in her and proving by his actions that he cared for her, gave her confidence he wasn't like the two men before who soured her view of commitment.

"I take that to mean you already know where this is going after our short dating period and acquaintance?" This was her first experience feeling this comfortable with a man that she could talk as if they were serious and not feel like the guy was going to disappear the next day.

He grinned, showing off the devilish smile that made her heart do back flips. "I knew I was going to get serious about you the first day we met. When you stood up to me even knowing I thought of you as a suspect. You didn't cower, you stood toe to toe with me and didn't back down. I thought that's one tough lady. One I wanted to know better."

"You really thought that the first time we met?" Do I dare tell him I had the same thoughts?

"Yes. When I went with the body to Coeur d'Alene, I told Bridget that I would be bringing you to Conor's wedding." He grinned, raised an eyebrow, and sipped his wine.

"You were that sure I'd agree?" She snorted. "Knowing that I may back out."

"You wouldn't. You're just as curious to meet my family as they are to meet you."

He had her there. "True. I've never met a whole family of sheep herders."

Ryan set the glass down and grabbed her around the waist. He slid her down on the porch swing . "We sheep herders have ways of bringing you cattle people to your senses."

Shandra froze. She drew in a deep breath and willed her eyes to remain on Ryan. He wasn't Floyd. Ryan's fingers ran across her ribs, and she couldn't stop the giggles. Ryan continued tickling her sides.

"Stop! Please stop!" She caught her breath. "I concede."

His fingers stopped their assault on her sides.

She stared up into his eyes. Eyes that smoldered with yearning and not craziness.

He leaned down, brushed his lips across hers, deepened the kiss for two long delicious minutes, and backed away from the porch swing.

"I'll let you know tomorrow what I find out about Lil's relations in Hafersville."

Before her head cleared and she registered Ryan had walked around the house, she heard his engine start up and the crunch of gravel under his tires.

"You're a tease, Ryan Greer!" she shouted and stretched her heated muscles. He'd set her body on fire with the smoldering look and the passionate kiss. And he'd proved he was nothing like the man who'd stole her innocence.

When the sound of his vehicle died away and Sheba barked at the back door, Shandra set to work, cleaning up the rest of the dinner mess, and went to bed.

A purple key chain floated around Shandra's head. She tried to grab the glittering object but it moved away. She followed, climbing up the mountain. The object stopped at her clay pocket where she'd found Johnny Clark's remains. It dropped to the ground. Shandra bent down to pick it up and found a ring. It appeared to be a wedding band with one purple stone. The inside glowed, revealing an inscription. Forever True, Johnny.

Shandra sat up. Sheba belly crawled up the bed to lay her head in Shandra's lap.

Stroking the furry head, Shandra replayed the dream. How had the key chain made it to the mountain? Did Lil drive her pickup to Sally's and back? Then the person who left the key with Johnny's body had to have been at the ranch. And the ring? Who had a good look at the ring when Johnny was at the café? Did it have a purple stone? Was there an inscription? It wasn't found with the body, where was it?

She grabbed the notebook by her bed and listed her questions and people to talk with in the morning.

~*~

Ryan drove back to the motel and took a long, cold shower. If he hadn't left when he did, he would have taken things much farther than Shandra was ready to go. When he stopped tickling her and stared down at her dark hair splayed across the porch swing, her hands flung above her head, her face glowing, and her eyes at half-mast, he'd been overcome with desire. Halfway into the kiss, he'd realized if he didn't pull back now, he could ruin his chances with Shandra. Someone in her past had hurt her. From her reactions it was more than an emotional hurt. It was physical. When he found out who it was, he was going to make sure the person paid.

He flipped through the TV channels. A Pro Rodeo popped onto the screen. There was no hesitation from Shandra when she said her father didn't die by accident. What isn't she telling me? He didn't want her looking into her father's death, but he had no way to keep her from doing it. The only consolation—he'd be there for her no matter what she found.

~*~

Ryan walked into the police station the next morning and sat down at Blane's desk and computer. He could have Hazel or even Cathleen dig up the records he wanted, but this way, if his suspicions didn't pan out, no one would know he'd suspected Lil's relatives of killing Johnny.

He punched in Lil's grandparents, read the obituaries, and discovered who had been their lawyer. The firm was still in town. Chances their lawyer still practiced were slight. He noted the law firm and closed the computer screen.

Hazel was once again seated at the dispatch desk.

"Isn't there anyone else who can do that job?" Ryan asked, stopping by dispatch on his way to the door.

"I like doing it. If I went home and sat around, I'd die."

"I doubt that. You're too young and active." Ryan held up the paper he'd wrote the firm's name on. "Do you have any idea if the lawyer from Yenks and Jarvis that drew up the Whitmires' wills is still alive?"

Hazel shook her head. "I know a lot about most people here but when it comes to who they used for legal stuff, I'm not much help. You could ask Sally Albright, Lil's momma's friend. Or try Jeffery Langley, he was friends with Ralph Whitmire. He's over at the Hafersville retirement home."

"Thanks, Hazel, you have been my best source of information on this case." Ryan left the building and climbed into his vehicle. He punched in

Shandra's phone number.

"Hello. I didn't expect to hear from you so soon." There was a pause. "You left in such a hurry I thought maybe I did something to upset you."

Ryan closed his eyes. *How do I tell her what happened without sounding like an adolescent pervert?*

"My leaving abruptly last night had nothing to do with you and everything to do with me. You want to take this attraction slow, and my body was racing onto stages you aren't ready for."

"Oh! I see."

Her breathy reply started his blood racing to areas that hadn't seen action in a while.

"Is that what you called to tell me?" Her tone held amusement.

"No. I found the law firm that drew up the Whitmires' wills. I don't know if there will be documents or anyone there who would remember anything, but Hazel suggested I ask Mrs. Albright, and a friend of Ralph Whitmire's. I thought you could ask Mrs. Albright and I'll check the law firm. We could meet for lunch and if neither one of us came up with anything, we could drive to Hafersville and ask the friend. He's in a retirement home there." Ryan mentally crossed his fingers she'd agree.

"I have some questions for Lil that came to me after a dream last night."

"Another visit from your grandmother?" Ryan asked. Most law officials didn't believe in clairvoyants or anything other than good hard facts, but having a mother who believed in the little people and seers, he wasn't as skeptical as most cops.

"She didn't appear, but it was all about the case and Lil. I'm sure she had a hand in it." There was a pause. "I still have trouble knowing you believe in her visiting me in my dreams. I haven't told anyone else because it makes me feel unstable even thinking about it."

"You're having more dreams and talk to me about them. You must be believing in them to do that. " Ryan appreciated that she trusted him enough to include him in her personal struggles.

"What time do you want to meet for lunch?"

"How about one? That will give you time to talk to Lil, drive down the mountain, and visit with Mrs. Albright." He wasn't sure what he'd do with that much time if the law firm was a bust, but he'd figure it out.

Chapter Twenty-four

Shandra hung up the phone and smiled. Now I know why Ryan left in such a hurry. She found his actions chivalrous and comical. I'm a grown woman. All he had to do was tell me he was getting horny and I'd have put space between us. He didn't have to run off like his pants were on fire. A laugh burst forth. Evidently his pants were on fire. And the thought didn't scare her. His actions proved her trust in him was valid.

She picked up her notebook of questions and headed to the barn, laughing all the way. She couldn't remember when she'd had such a good laugh. I don't doubt with Ryan around there would be many more.

At the barn, she walked straight to Lil's room. Light shone under the door proving she hadn't started her chores.

Shandra knocked on the door.

"Come in," Lil said, opening the door.

Lewis was curled around Lil's neck like an orange fur stole. Lil wore her signature purple. Today it was a pair of corduroy pants and a flowered, long-sleeved shirt.

"I have some questions that came up when Ryan and I were talking about you and Johnny last night." Shandra took the one chair by the table.

Lil sat down on the side of the bed and closed her eyes. "What kind of questions?"

"The key chain with purple stones and your name. What keys were on it?" She'd start with the easy questions.

"I had an old pickup that Pappy gave me when I turned twenty. The key chain had the key to it and the house."

"Did you drive that pickup when you went to Sally's after you lost the baby?" She hated bringing up sad times, but she didn't know how else to ask the questions.

"Yes. It was parked in the back of Sally's until I drove home."

"Did you leave the keys in the truck when you arrived home?" Someone had to have taken the keys from the vehicle and dropped them in with the body.

"I don't…I usually left them in the pickup when it was parked here. No one ever stole any of the vehicles. They all had the keys in them." Lil's face was a study in concentration.

"Do you remember if they were there the next time you drove the pickup?" Shandra held her breath, willing the woman to remember something that would help steer them in the direction of the murderer.

Lil shook her head. "I was just getting up the nerve to tell Gran why I'd been at Sally's for a week when Uncle Jerome arrived yelling the barn was on fire. We all went to the barn and put the fire out. Then Pappy and Uncle Jerome looked around and called the police. Before I knew it, they were hauling me down to the station and questioning me about starting the fire. After the fight, losing the baby, and being hauled in like a criminal, I didn't leave this mountain for months. So I can't say when or if I even thought about the key chain being missing."

Sympathy for the woman oozed from Shandra. An event that should have made her life wonderful, had instead, ruined the life she'd dreamed of.

"Ryan is looking into your grandparents' wills. Do you remember anything about their wishes?" Shandra hoped Lil had been more business savvy back then than she'd proved so far.

"All I knew was the ranch was going to me. But when they became ill and needed medical treatment, I talked them into selling to pay for their care."

"How did your uncle feel about that?" She had to find someone who had it out for Lil.

"He didn't like the idea of ithe ranch going to me. He wanted it, so he could sell. If Gran and Pappy had been healthier toward the end, and we hadn't needed to sell, I would have never sold the ranch. They knew that. I spent months telling them I didn't need to own the ranch. That it wouldn't do me any good if they left me with huge medical expenses. That finally sunk in. They agreed to sell."

"What happened to that money? What they made from the sale?" Shandra didn't think that money had anything to do with Johnny's murder since the sale happened years later, but she needed to know.

"Most of it went to pay for Gran and Pappy. Then Pappy died." She brushed at a tear. "Then Gran." She sighed, deep and long. "Then the rest was left to me." Lil's face reddened. "Uncle Jerome threw a fit. He said he deserved more than me. He went to Mr. Yenks, my grandparents' lawyer. I heard he yelled at the lawyer for letting Gran and Pappy leave everything to me." She shook her head. "By that time there wasn't that much. I kept ten thousand and gave the rest to Uncle Jerome to keep him quiet."

Shandra latched onto the last statement. "Quiet? What do you mean?"

"He and Aunt May started up again about how I tried to burn down the barn and brought up dumb stuff I did as a kid but made it sound like I was doing that stuff as an adult. You know, trying to make me sound crazy. Then Marti going around calling me Crazy Lil all the time got others saying the same. At first I stayed away from town and people as much as I could. Then this place sold, again, and I tried to come back and work for them. But word got to them I was called Crazy Lil and I had a heck of a time trying to get work anywhere.

The money I'd kept was used up, and I took to sleeping on the mountain."

Shandra rose, crossed the short span between them, and hugged Lil. How could anyone turn on family? Her uncle sounded like the black sheep of the family.

"I'm sorry you've led such a solitary life. And I'm glad you were here when I bought the ranch. You have been a good worker and I hope from here on out a good friend."

Lil's eyes filled with tears. "You are the first person besides Sally to want to be my friend since Johnny died. I appreciated when you hired me and I appreciate your friendship."

Shandra hugged the woman tighter then released. "I need to head to town. I'm meeting Ryan for lunch." She stood and walked to the door.

"I saw him leave last night. He was in a hurry. Thought maybe you two had a falling out."

The question in Lil's voice made Shandra smile. Why he left in a hurry was between Ryan and herself.

"Yeah, he had a call and had to leave." A little white lie, considering the reason for his departure, seemed just.

Shandra patted Sheba on the head as she walked out into the summer sunshine. It would be a beautiful day. One she should have spent working on her art, but finding the person who had ruined Lil's life was top priority.

~*~

Ryan sat across the desk from Rodney Yenks, the third generation to work at the law firm of

Yenks and Jarvis.

"You don't look old enough to have handled the estate of Ralph and Virginia Whitmire," said Ryan, watching the man across from him lean back in his chair to show off his fancy vest under the equally expensive suit coat.

"No, they were my grandfather's clients and were passed down to my father. I believe he was the executor of their estate." Yenks peered at him through Clark Kent glasses. But the wispy, fair-haired man was far from the iconic image of Superman.

"Would your firm happen to have their wills and any preceding wills on record?" Ryan didn't like the way the man's hands couldn't seem to light in one place.

"We would if the building we were previously in hadn't burned down ten years ago. I'm afraid that information hadn't been scanned into a database before the fire."

Damn! The only upside to the information was a road trip with Shandra.

"Was the fire accidental or ruled arson?" He didn't see a person setting fire to the records before Johnny Clark's body had been found, but the cop in him was curious.

"Wiring. The building was one of the first built in Huckleberry and the one least updated." Mr. Yenks leaned forward. "Why all these questions about the Whitmire estate? Does it have anything to do with the body found on the ranch? I've heard that crazy granddaughter of theirs got everything and she knew the cowboy whose bones were found."

Ryan couldn't stop his answer, even if it was unwarranted. "Right now everyone in Huckleberry is a suspect. Including you." Ryan stood, extended his hand, and shook. "Thank you for the information."

He left the law firm and headed to Sally Albright's. He didn't see any reason he couldn't join Shandra when she questioned the woman.

Chapter Twenty-five

Shandra pulled up to Sally's house and found Ryan sitting in his SUV. By the time she stopped and exited her vehicle, Ryan waited for her at the sidewalk leading up to Sally's house.

"What are you doing here?" she asked, not even trying to keep the joy from showing on her face.

"The law firm's building burned down ten years ago. Nothing was scanned in. So, no luck there. I figured we could talk with Sally together." He waved her up the walkway.

"Watch your step on the porch. This place hasn't seen repairs in a long time." Shandra picked her way across the precarious cracking boards and gaps and knocked on the door.

Ryan was so close behind her she could feel his

heat.

"You're a bit close don't you think?" she said over her shoulder.

"It's either stand on the same boards you are, or stand on the sidewalk."

She giggled.

The door opened.

"Now you're bringing guests?" Sally asked, with a slight smile before retreating into the house, dragging her oxygen behind her.

Shandra led the way into the small living room. What had once been neat and tidy was now littered with half-packed boxes.

"You're moving?" Shandra asked, taking in the carefully wrapped knick-knacks nestled in the boxes.

"Yes, my niece has been after me to move closer to her. Now that Lil has you, I feel I can move away." Tears glistened in the old woman's eyes.

"I'm happy you trust me to be her friend." Shandra sat on her usual chair. Ryan pulled a straight-backed chair from the kitchen and sat beside her. "Mrs. Albright—,"

"Sally, please," the woman offered.

"Sally, this is Detective Ryan Greer with the Sheriff's Department. We have some more questions about Lil's family." Shandra introduced the two.

"Ma'am, pleased to meet you," Ryan said, tipping his head.

"You aren't anything like the deputy I called years ago to help me with my drunk husband." The older woman's cheeks blushed. "He was as round as he was tall and not especially easy to look at or talk to."

Shandra ducked her head so neither one could see the smile on her lips. She cleared her throat to ask the first question. "Did you know about the Whitmires' wills giving Lil the ranch?"

The woman's eyes narrowed slightly. "Yes, I told Lil she was being too generous to those old people when she talked them into selling her inheritance. The way they treated her like a slave instead of a grandchild, I thought she should have put them in a nursing home and let Jerome pay for their care."

"Jerome had money to do that?" The way Lil had talked, Shandra thought Jerome sounded desperate for money.

Sally nodded her head. "He married well. His wife had the purse strings. She thought the world of Ralph and Virginia until they took in Lil." She tipped her head coquettishly. "She didn't want the world to know, but she told Jerome if he brought Lil into their home she'd leave him."

"Jerome's wife? Why didn't she want Lil? She was just a child when her parents died." Everything Shandra was learning about Jerome and his wife wasn't painting them to be a very nice couple.

"May, Jerome's wife, was a cousin to Lil's mom. She was ticked off that she didn't get the brother who was to inherit the ranch." Sally coughed and sucked on her oxygen.

Shandra studied the woman and glanced at

Ryan. She could see he was trying to puzzle things together as well.

"But I would think she'd take in the child who would inherit," Ryan said.

Sally turned her fading gaze on Ryan. "After the accident, Jerome believed he was next in line for the ranch. When Ralph announced the ranch was going to Lil, she was around twenty."

"What happened then? When Jerome and May discovered the ranch was going to Lil?" Shandra had a feeling she knew the answer.

"That's when Jerome cut off his ties with Ralph and Virginia. From what I've gleaned over the years, May and Janine, her daughter, put the chasm between Lil and her grandparents, and Jerome."

"You said Janine, her daughter. Don't you mean their daughter?" Ryan asked.

"No, Janine is May's daughter from a previous marriage." Sally stared at Ryan as if he was a particularly slow student.

"Where is the first husband?" Ryan asked.

"She was a widow when Jerome met her," Sally said, straightening her clear oxygen tubes.

Shandra was losing track of her thoughts with all the new information. "How did they meet?"

"Lil's mom invited May to stay with them at the ranch for a weekend. Jerome fell hard for May, and they were married in less than a year." Sally fiddled with her oxygen tube.

"They never had children—May and Jerome?" Shandra asked.

"No. Lil's mom told me she felt responsible for Jerome not having a family of his own." Sally picked up a photo. She handed it to Shandra. "This is a photo of the whole family the weekend before the crash that killed Lucy and Paul."

Shandra closely examined the faces of the people in the photo. Ryan leaned closer and studied the photograph.

Lil was about ten, her face was glowing. The smile on her face sparkled in her eyes. A woman with her hand on Lil's shoulder could have been taken out of the photos of Lil at that age. The man with his arm around the woman's shoulders must have been Lil's father. The older couple in the middle would be Virginia and Ralph Whitmire. The three to their left looked uncomfortable. The girl, the same size and age as Lil was frowning, her arms crossed. The woman was stately and held herself straight-rigid. The man, who must be Jerome, leaned as if he wanted to put an arm around the woman but feared rejection.

From the photo she didn't think Jerome led a very happy life. Had he gone to the ranch that night to try and mend fences with his parents?

"But Jerome was at the ranch the night Lil went back after being with you for a week." Shandra wondered if the call Janine made had been to her father or her mother. But what would either care that Lil was getting married?

"Thank you, Sally. You've been a valuable source of knowledge about Lil and her family." Ryan stood. "Good luck with the move."

He held out his hand to help Shandra to her feet. She peered into his eyes. Something that was said had triggered his hasty departure. What had she missed? She had more questions.

"Sally, I'll let Lil know you're moving, so she can come see you before you leave." Shandra leaned down and gave the woman a hug.

"Thank you, I'd like to say good-bye to her. Let yourselves out."

Shandra followed Ryan's long strides out of the house and out to their cars. "What did you hear that has you in a hurry?"

"Hop in my vehicle. We'll grab burgers at the drive-thru and head to Hafersville. It's what she didn't say. Something in the will has to be the clue to why Johnny was murdered and not Lil." Ryan held the passenger door open for her.

Shandra climbed in and waited for Ryan to get behind the steering wheel. Once he was settled she said, "It did sound like greed and jealousy could be the reasons behind the murder."

She sat rewinding the conversation with Sally as Ryan ordered burgers and shakes. When they were on the road to Hafersville, she asked, "Do you think they were also the ones behind spreading the rumors? The ones about Lil being crazy? If they locked Lil up, that would leave them as the soul beneficiaries."

"The only thing I know for sure. This case revolves around Lil, even though she wasn't the murder victim."

~*~

Ryan parked in the visitor section of the Hafersville retirement home. He escorted Shandra into the building. At the front desk, they asked for

Mr. Jeffery Langley.

"He's in room twenty-four but don't be surprised if he throws you out," the nurse said, hurrying off to answer a light blinking on the console from room fifty-one.

Ryan glanced at Shandra. Her eyes were focused down the hall and her lips were set in a line of determination. He had an inkling they wouldn't leave here until they'd learned something from Mr. Langley.

At the door of room twenty-four, Shandra put a hand on his arm. "Why don't you let me go in first? Kind of break the ice."

He didn't want to send her in alone given the nurse's comment, but it made more sense than him barging in and possibly setting the man off. "Ok, but I'll be listening at the door in case he gets violent."

She stood on her tiptoes and kissed his cheek. "My hero."

Before Ryan's ego had time to deflate, Shandra disappeared into the room. He stood at the door listening.

"Mr. Langley? I'm Shandra Higheagle. I'm here with a friend. We'd like to ask you questions about Ralph and Virginia Whitmire."

"What? Who are you? What do you want?" bellowed a voice.

Great. The man didn't even remember his best friend. Ryan took a step inside the door.

"Speak up, I didn't feel like shoving a hearing aid in my ear this morning," the man bellowed. He didn't seem to know how to use a normal voice.

"I'm Shandra. My friend, Detective Greer, would like to come in and visit with you, too. Is that all right?" She'd elevated her voice to just lower than a yell.

Great. The whole nursing home would hear their conversation. It wasn't the way Ryan liked to handle an investigation. But they didn't have a choice if the old man was hard of hearing. He wondered how Shandra managed to make her voice sound calm and soothing while speaking so loudly. The man bellowed like she was a mile away.

"I guess." A pause. "You said he was a detective?"

"Yes, we're investigating a murder that occurred on the Whitmire Ranch on Huckleberry Mountain," Shandra said sweetly and motioned with her hand for him to enter.

Ryan stepped into the room. The man's gaze flew off of Shandra and zeroed in on him.

"Who are you?"

"I'm Detective Greer with the Weippe County Sheriff's Department." When the man started to tilt his head as if he couldn't hear, Ryan raised his voice. "We would like to ask you questions about the Whitmire family. We were told you were friends with Ralph." Ryan walked slowly over to where Shandra stood about six feet from a recliner. In the chair sat a man who had once been a hulk of a man. His stooped shoulders were as wide as the chair back. He was neither fat nor too thin. Whether his muscles now failed him as much as his hearing they could soon find out if he became riled.

"Whitmire you say?" He appeared to be searching the recesses of his mind.

Ryan scanned the room and found a photograph of the man in the chair with Ralph Whitmire on what looked to be a fishing trip. He crossed the room and tapped the photo. "This man. Ralph Whitmire."

"Why didn't you say Jackass and Ginny? Jackass and I've been friends since grade school."

Shandra sputtered and giggled. "Jackass? How did he get that name?"

Ryan had trouble keeping a straight face, too. He wanted to hear how this man got his nickname and why it was the one the old coot in the chair remembered.

"When we were kids, Jackass could fool people into thinking there was a jackass in their garden or garage, or wherever they wouldn't want one, by braying. We all thought it was great fun, but when he married Ginny…well the name fit even better."

"That is a good story," Shandra said, settling on the straight-backed chair not too far from Jeffery. "But Jenny is the name of a female donkey not Ginny."

"Jenny, Ginny, close enough," The old man said and smiled, showing off missing teeth and adding a gleam to his eyes.

"Do you remember Jackass and Ginny's granddaughter?" Shandra asked.

"Little Lil? Yeah. She was a sparkler until her mom and dad died. Jackass was too strict with her. He should have let the girl out more." The man's expression softened as he talked about Lil.

"We wondered if Jackass ever talked to you about his will," Ryan offered, standing beside Shandra.

"Hell, we talked about everything. The girls we nailed, the price of cigarettes, and whether or not that piece-of-shit son of his would ever think of something besides easy money."

"You're talking about Jerome and not Lil's father?" Shandra asked.

"Yeah, Jerome was always trying to make money and losing more than his wife was willing to shell out to save him."

"Is that why they left him out of the will?" Shandra leaned forward.

"The ranch was going to the oldest, Paul, until he died. Then they put together a trust and named their lawyer as executor. If Lil married before her thirty-fifth birthday, she received the ranch. If she didn't marry, she got it when Jackass and Ginny died." He shook his head. "Fool girl talked them into selling to pay for their growing medical expenses. I doubt she ended up with much by the time Jackass, and then Ginny was buried."

"Actually, when Jerome started rumors about Lil, she gave him most of the money to shut him up," Shandra stated.

Ryan stared at Shandra. "Why did she do that? A blackmailer never stops."

"She gave it all to him, there was no more to give and he knew it." Shandra's eyes glinted with anger.

Ryan studied her. He'd not witnessed this level

of outrage from her before. "Did Lil know about the trust?" he asked, waiting for the two in the room to respond.

Shandra shook her head. "I don't think so. She didn't mention it. Only that she was to get the ranch when her grandparents died. I think she believed there was only a will."

Langley nodded his head. "Jackass didn't tell Lil about the trust. He didn't want her running off and marrying the first guy that looked her way just to get the ranch. Even though I told him Lil wasn't like Jerome. She would have seen to their needs and kept that ranch for her children."

Shandra nodded. "She loves that ranch. I own the ranch now and Lil works for me."

"That's good. Real good," Langley said. "She was a good kid. Didn't deserve being treated like a prisoner."

"How is that?" Ryan asked, becoming more interested in Lil's upbringing.

"They didn't let her go off the ranch except to school. When she wasn't at school she was working alongside Jackass mending fences, moving cattle, whatever chore needed done." He scratched his head with long, gnarled fingers. "That was the only thing Jackass and I ever quarreled about. How he didn't let that girl grow some wings and learn to fly."

Shandra touched the man's arm, drawing his attention to her. "What did Jackass and Ginny think of Johnny Clark, the rodeo announcer Lil was dating?"

"They liked him well enough, but were worried about him being an alcoholic."

"Do you think if he asked Lil to marry him, they would have allowed it?" Shandra asked.

Ryan moved his gaze between the two. Shandra waited, practically holding her breath. The old man seemed to be studying on the question.

Chapter Twenty-six

"I think if Lil said she loved the man, and he proved to be stable, they would have given their blessing. I know Ginny wanted Lil to find a man and be happy," Mr. Langley said. "And it would have done the girl good to get away from that ranch for a while."

Shandra released the air clogged in her lungs. She'd wondered if maybe Jackass-Ralph had killed Johnny to keep Lil around, but from Mr. Langley's comment, she mentally scratched him off the list of suspects.

"Thank you Mr. Langley. You've told us what we needed to know." Ryan touched her shoulder. "Come on. We've heard what we needed."

Shandra gently patted the old man's hand, gnarled and crippled by arthritis. "It was a pleasure to meet you. Our visit with you was very helpful." She stood and walked to the door.

"You two come back again. I don't get many visitors."

The wistfulness on the man's face tugged at Shandra.

"I'll stop in the next time I come to Hafersville." She walked out the door and leaned on Ryan. "I don't know what the nurse was talking about, he's a nice old man."

Ryan put an arm around her shoulders. "I have a feeling you bring out the best in everyone you meet."

"No, with my background and volatile step-father, I learned to judge people before I start talking with them. If you keep the conversation on what they like or what brings them fond memories, you can learn a lot and make them happy." Shandra straightened. "I'm thinking we need to have a chat with Jerome Whitmire."

"I had the same idea." Ryan held the passenger door open for her.

She slid in and waited for him to walk around the front of the vehicle.

Once he was behind the steering wheel, Ryan pulled out his phone and dialed. "Cathleen, I need the address for Jerome Whitmire in Hafersville." His face wrinkled into a frown. "No, I don't want to go in with you and Bridget for a wedding gift."

He rolled his eyes and shrugged. "Because I already have a gift for them."

Ryan started the engine. "Text me the address." He pressed a button and put the phone back in the holster on his belt.

"You call your sister to get addresses for you?" Shandra wondered at the budget of the sheriff's department.

"She works as a dispatcher for the county. When she isn't answering the calls, she pulls up information on the computer." Ryan backed out of the parking space. "Sometimes having a sister in the workplace is a pain in the ass. But there are times when it's nice to have family there when you come in from a tough assignment."

Shandra knew he was close with his siblings. Some days she yearned for a sibling to bounce family strife off of, but as an only child she didn't have that luxury. She'd thought about connecting with cousins on Daddy's side. *I should really do that.*

Ryan's phone beeped. He pulled it out, looked at the message, and turned the car left onto the road. "He lives on the high-class side of town."

"That makes sense given what we know about his wife's money." Shandra studied the downtown area. She'd only driven to Hafersville once since moving to the ranch. It was a quaint town that wasn't overrun by tourists like Huckleberry. But tourists came on vacations to spend money and that's where her art needed to be.

A sign over an old brick building said Whitmire Hardware. "Do you think he's at the store?" She pointed to the building.

Ryan pulled into a parking slot. "Let's see."

Shandra climbed out of the vehicle before Ryan

came to her side to open the door. She enjoyed his chivalry, but there were times when she wanted out of the car faster than he could round the hood of the car. This was one of them. She had to look Jerome Whitmire in the eyes and see if he lied about Lil and the night Johnny died.

There were two older men in blue vests. One was helping a customer and the other was standing behind the counter.

Ryan walked up to the counter. He motioned to the badge attached to his belt and said, "We're looking for Jerome Whitmire."

The man's eyes widened. "Mr. Whitmire went home about thirty minutes ago after he received a call."

Shandra peered into Ryan's eyes. Who called him?

"Does he get calls often and leave during the day?" Ryan asked.

"Once in a while his wife will call and he'll run out of here. This one wasn't his wife." The man shook his head.

"But it was a woman?" Ryan asked.

The man nodded vigorously.

"Come on." Ryan grasped Shandra's arm and practically ran to the vehicle.

"Why are you hurrying? We don't know where he went." Shandra climbed into his SUV and slammed the door as Ryan pulled away from the curb.

"If his car isn't parked at home, we ask his family where he might be. But my first guess is he's in Huckleberry. Someone there got his attention."

Ryan dialed the police radio in his car. "Hazel? Look up the license and make of Jerome Whitmire's vehicle. Have Blane cruise around town looking for it. Tell him not to engage but let me know where he is. Over"

Ryan had a bad feeling about Whitmire rabbiting. He was either running or he was out to take care of someone who knew he killed Johnny Clark.

The SUV sat on its nose as he slammed on the brakes when he nearly missed the road to the Whitmire house. He turned up a long drive lined with Chinese maple and stopped in front of a large log home. The house appeared to be new compared to the rest of the town.

Shandra's knuckles were white from gripping the arm rest.

"Sorry about that. I think someone may be in danger. We need to discover where Whitmire is as quickly as possible." He exited the vehicle.

Shandra scrambled out and followed him up the walkway. "I understand. Sort of. You believe Jerome killed Johnny?"

"Yes. To keep Lil from marrying. I think he was hoping to get back in his parents' good graces." Ryan raised his hand and rapped on the door.

A teen-aged girl answered the door. "May I help you?"

Ryan tapped his badge. "Detective Greer with the Weippe County Sheriff. I'd like to speak with Jerome Whitmire."

"He's not here." The girl started to close the

door.

Ryan shoved his weight against the door, pushing the girl backward. "I need to talk with Mrs. Whitmire then."

"My grandmother's busy." The girl tried to shove back, but her teenage body was no match for his bulk.

Ryan shoved the door open and stood inside. "Tell her it could be the difference between her going to jail as an accessory or just answering questions."

"Heidi, let the man in. I have nothing to be worried about."

A tall slender woman in clothes Ryan was pretty sure cost a fortune, sauntered down the hall toward the entry. Sparkly jewelry on her ears, arms, and fingers glittered in the sunlight from the open door.

Ryan grasped Shandra's arm, drawing her into the house. He wanted her close by to keep her out of harm should things get ugly.

The older woman pivoted on a silver shoe and headed into what looked to be a living area.

Ryan followed.

Once they all stood inside the room, Ryan tapped the badge on his belt. "I'm Detective Greer of the Weippe County—"

The woman waved her hand. "I heard who you were. What do you want with my husband?" She remained standing.

Ryan had met this type before when he worked homicide in Chicago. They tried to make you feel inferior by standing and trying to take over the conversation.

"We need to know why he was at his parents' house the night the barn caught fire," Ryan said. Better to start with the questions that would catch the lies than come out and state what he really wanted to know.

"That was a long time ago. You can't possibly expect me to remember that far back." Mrs. Whitmire waved bejeweled hands.

"It could make the difference between you going to jail with your husband or just him going to jail." Ryan knew how this type thought. They'd always give up someone else to save their skin.

"I'll have to think about it. It was nearly twenty-five—"

"Thirty. Thirty years ago," Shandra said.

Warmth expanded his chest. Shandra knew when to be quiet and when to interject. She was as perceptive as any good detective.

"Really? That long ago?" Mrs. Whitmire finally settled onto a fancy couch, leaving them to stand or find seating on two matching chairs.

Ryan motioned to the chairs. Shandra sat in the one farthest from the woman. Ryan took the one closest and pulled out his notepad.

"The date was September eighth in nineteen-eighty-four," he read from the notes he took from the police report.

"I can't believe you expect me to remember what happened thirty years ago." The woman took the offensive.

"I would think you would remember a fire at

your in-laws' ranch," Shandra said, in a soft, un-accusing tone.

"I do remember Jerome saying something about the barn, and he'd thought our niece had started it." The woman's eyes opened wider. "Is that what you mean? The night Jerome visited and saw Lil coming from the barn, and then the barn going up in flames?"

Ryan wasn't convinced the woman wasn't being theatrical on purpose. "He was positive it was Lil?"

"He said it was a young, blonde woman. Who else fitting that description would have been at the Whitmire Ranch besides Lil?" Mrs. Whitmire folded her hands in her lap.

"That's a lovely ring you have Mrs. Whitmire," Shandra said, standing. "May I look at it?"

The woman smiled. "It was a gift from Jerome."

Chapter Twenty-seven

Shandra's heart pounded in her chest. The ring had one purple stone set in the band. The piece of jewelry was exactly like the ring in her dream. She was surprised when the woman didn't hesitate to drop it in her hand.

Her fingers shook as she tipped the ring to see if there was an inscription.

Forever True, J.

Her heart went from over beating to a screeching halt. They'd found the murderer. Jerome Whitmire. Now to prove it.

She cleared her throat to keep her excitement from coming through. "Thank you, Mrs. Whitmire that is a beautiful ring. Do you happen to know where your husband purchased it? I'd love to get one for myself with a different color stone."

She glanced at Ryan. He raised an eyebrow in question but remained quiet.

"I don't know where Jerome purchased this. He gave it to me right after his parents moved into a retirement home." She slid the ring back on her finger and glared at Ryan. "I would think if you wanted to know the truth about the fire in the barn you should speak with Crazy Lil." The woman sniffed. "She should have been locked up years ago."

"Why do you say that?" Shandra couldn't keep the contempt from her voice. Why would anyone want to lock up a perfectly sane person?

"She was a loner, dressed funny, and she tried to burn down a barn. Isn't that enough reasons?" The woman stared at Shandra as if she needed to be locked up as well.

"Those aren't even close to good reasons. I think you and your husband had other reasons to want Lil out of the way. I think you were hoping to inherit the Whitmire Ranch." Shandra didn't spare a glance at Ryan. She was sure he wasn't happy with her spilling what they knew. But the woman had no right saying how Lil should be treated. May Whitmire only had dollar signs driving her and not the sweet nature of Lil.

"Of course, we hoped to inherit the ranch after the tragic accident that took Lil's parents. Then Ralph and Virginia lost their minds and set up that trust for Lil. How could a single woman run a place like that? Especially, with Ralph getting sicker and sicker each year. He wouldn't be able to help her."

Ryan cleared his throat. "But the trust read Lil

would receive the ranch at thirty-five if she was married. A husband would solve the problems you stated."

Shandra smiled at Ryan. She wanted to say something but felt she'd already overstepped her bounds.

"Well, yes, there was that. But the girl wasn't even dating." Mrs. Whitmire didn't look at either one of them when she said this.

"But she was seeing someone. Johnny Clark, the rodeo announcer," Shandra said sweetly.

"He was nothing. He proved it by dropping out of her life." Again, Mrs. Whitmire stared at the wall behind them and not at them.

"How do you know he dropped out of her life? Moments ago you said she didn't even have a boyfriend?" Ryan leaned forward in his chair.

"Well, I knew of the cowboy. Ralph and Virginia called Jerome the night of the fire. They were worried because Lil had been gone for a week. They said Sally Albright called and said Lil was with her, but they feared Lil had run off with that cowboy." The woman sniffed as if she'd caught the stench of something foul. "That Albright woman was always sticking her nose into business that wasn't hers. Saying Lil's mom asked her to. How could Lil's mom ask her to unless she knew she was going to die?" The woman's eyes were round and emitted disbelief.

"Surely, as a parent you've asked friends to watch over your children should something happen to you." Shandra knew her mother had asked her best friend to watch over her daughter should something happen before Shandra was an adult.

"My children were well taken care of and it would continue if something happened to me." Mrs. Whitmire was the epitome of an ice parent.

"So that's why your husband was at the ranch the night the barn caught fire? To help his parents locate Lil? Even though she was at the ranch." The skepticism in Ryan's voice couldn't have been lost on the woman.

"Yes. By the time Jerome made the trip all the way to the ranch, Lil had returned." The woman nodded.

"Did she say where she'd been?" Ryan continued to question.

Shandra was happy to see how the woman responded and stayed out of the way.

"She'd been at that Albright woman's house."

"Like the woman had told her grandparents." Ryan stated.

"Yes." The woman huffed the answer.

"Why would she set fire to the barn if she'd just returned?" Ryan asked.

"I don't know. Who knows why unstable people do what they do." She stared at her nails.

"The only reason Jerome went to the ranch was to soothe his parents and help to find Lil?" Ryan asked.

"Yes."

Shandra had a question. "Why did your daughter Janine call home that night? Was it to tell you that Johnny Clark was proposing to Lil?" She didn't stop to wait for an answer. "While Lil didn't know about the marriage clause in the trust I bet your daughter did. After all, how else could you keep the two cousins at odds if you didn't fuel the controversy?"

"Who are you?" the woman snarled.

"Lil's employer and the person who dug up Johnny Clark's body."

"No!" Mrs. Whitmire covered her mouth and shook her head.

"No, what?" Ryan pounced on her exclamation and loss of composure.

"He was only supposed to pay Johnny off. Make him disappear and not come back." Mrs. Whitmire slumped back against the sofa.

"Who was only supposed to pay Johnny off?" Ryan pursued.

"Jerome. When Janine called with the news Johnny was showing off a ring and planning to marry Lil, I sent Jerome to find Johnny and pay him off. A rodeo cowboy would take the money and run." She shook her head. "Jerome returned late that night. He said he'd paid off Johnny and then saw Lil running from the burning barn. He said he had the police pull her in. So we'd get the ranch because she'd never marry and we could spread the word she was crazy."

"Mrs. Whitmire, Johnny never left that ranch. He's been buried on the mountain for thirty years. Where can we find your husband?" Ryan stood, flipping his notepad closed.

"I don't know. He should be at work."

Shandra stood. "We came from there. They said

he received a call from a woman and left in a hurry."

"Then I have no idea where he could be." She waved her hand. "Leave. I'm not feeling well."

"Thank you for your time." Ryan waved Shandra to exit.

Once they were sitting in Ryan's vehicle, Shandra turned to him. "I think Jerome Whitmire is the murderer. That ring I asked about. I saw it in my dream. Only the message engraved on the inside was *Forever True, Johnny*. This ring had *Forever True, J.* He could have had the rest of Johnny removed by a jeweler."

Ryan started the engine. "We need to ask the one witness to the ring what it looked like. Maybe by the time we get to Huckleberry, Blane will have found Jerome's car."

Chapter Twenty-eight

Ryan pulled into Huckleberry and parked in front of the City Recorder's Office. He was pretty sure given all they knew about Martha, she would be able to describe the ring Johnny had been showing off at the café. What he didn't understand was Janine had been present at the café at the time. Why hadn't she made the connection between the ring Johnny was showing off and the one her father gave her mother?

Shandra's door flew open the moment he put the vehicle in park. He hurried to catch up to her at the door.

"Don't rush in there and start questioning Martha." Ryan put a hand on Shandra's shoulder to keep her from charging into the building. "Be calm and act as if we don't have all the information we do."

Shandra nodded, but he felt her tension.

He opened the door, and they walked in.

Martha looked up from her desk. "Hello." Her greeting wasn't as cheerful as the first time he'd stepped into this office.

"Mrs. Samples, could you describe the ring Johnny Clark was planning to give Lil the night he came into the café?" Ryan pulled out his notepad.

Her gaze flit from him to Shandra and back to him. "Why do you need to know that?"

"It's evidence." Ryan said flatly, hoping to keep the woman from dodging the question.

"That was a long time ago." She countered.

"But when a woman looks at a wedding ring even if it isn't her own, she admires it," Shandra said.

Ryan wondered if Shandra wanted a wedding ring of her own as he watched Martha.

Her face reddened. "He only flashed it. I didn't get a good look."

"What did you see?" Ryan persisted.

"There was a stone."

"Stone? Not a diamond?" Ryan didn't want her to come back and say he put words in her mouth. She had to say the color.

"No diamond. A purple stone. Johnny said he chose a purple stone because Lil liked his purple scarf so much." Martha crinkled her nose. "She wore that stupid purple scarf until it practically rotted on her neck. And now she wears all those purple clothes. It's crazy. She's crazy."

"It's not crazy for a person to mourn the loss of

a love and a life she'd been dreaming of." The sadness in Shandra's voice drew Ryan's gaze. Lil's plight moved her deeply.

"Did Johnny mention anything about engraving on the ring?" He hadn't wanted to ask this leading question but Martha said she barely saw the ring. If she'd held it in her hands, he would have asked if she'd noticed anything else about the ring.

"He said it was engraved but didn't say what it said." Martha narrowed her eyes. "What's with all these questions about a ring?"

"You'll learn about it when we apprehend Johnny's murderer." Ryan flipped his notepad closed. He pivoted toward the door. Shandra's boot heels tapped a quick cadence behind him.

At the vehicle, he leaned against the hood. "Now to find Jerome Whitmire." He snatched his phone from his belt and dialed the Huckleberry police station.

"Hi Hazel. Has Blane found Jerome Whitmire's car?"

"No. It's like the man disappeared. Do you suspect him of Johnny Clark's death?" Hazel's tone was more challenging than inquisitive.

"Let's just say we are gathering strong evidence against him. Let me know as soon as he's spotted."

"Will do."

Ryan punched the off button and stared up and down the street.

"Still no sign of him?" Shandra asked.

"Blane hasn't seen a thing." Ryan's gaze

landed on Ruthie's restaurant. "How about dinner and I'll return you to your car?"

Shandra didn't want to eat, she wanted to find Jerome. If he left the hardware store in a hurry after a phone call from a woman and he wasn't to be found, he either knew they were on to him, or he knew they were getting close and he was covering his tracks.

But she couldn't think of what to do to find him.

"Might as well. We're stuck at the moment." She fell into step beside Ryan as they walked to Ruthie's.

"If May didn't call Jerome, what other woman did, and why did he run out so quickly after that call?" She wasn't really asking Ryan, just musing out loud.

"Who are the women we believe are involved?" Ryan asked, accepting her random rattling.

"May Whitmire, Janine Whitmire, Tracy Gilley, Martha Samples."

"Don't forget Lil," Ryan said.

"But you aren't still considering her the killer are you?" Shandra was pretty sure he no longer believed Lil killed the man she loved.

"No. I consider her a victim."

Shandra's heart skipped a beat. Ryan understood Lil was one of the victims in this crime. But it also meant she was still a victim.

"We have to go to my ranch!" Shandra spun on her heel jogging back to Ryan's vehicle.

Ryan caught up to her as she climbed into the passenger seat. He hopped behind the wheel and started the SUV.

"Why your ranch?"

"Like you said, Lil is the victim. What if she called her uncle after I questioned her about the night the barn burned? She could have called asking questions. Questions he didn't want asked." Shandra clutched the arm rest as Ryan raced out of Huckleberry and up the county road toward her ranch. "My dreams have been telling me Lil was alone. I thought it meant because she lost Johnny and the baby, but I think it's because her family, what's left of it, is also her enemy."

"You think Jerome was at the ranch that night because he followed Johnny? And when Johnny wouldn't take the bribe to leave, Jerome killed him?" Ryan asked.

"That's the way my thinking is headed. He had access to Lil's pickup to get the key chain. He said she started the barn on fire. He probably did that to get her off the premises while he buried the body." Shandra was picturing it all in her mind. Yes, Jerome murdered Johnny.

Their heads banged against the roof of the vehicle a couple times as Ryan pushed the limits over the bumpy lane leading into her ranch.

A mile from the ranch, he slowed down. "We don't want to give away our approach if Jerome has a gun on Lil."

Ryan's statement sent a chill down Shandra's spine. He'd killed once. He could have already killed Lil.

Before breaking into the clearing of the ranch

buildings, Ryan shut off the vehicle. "Come on. We'll go on foot from here."

Shandra slipped out of the vehicle, scanning the area for Sheba. If she saw a man with a gun, she'd be cowering under something. For her size and bravado she was worthless as a guard dog. There was a car she didn't know parked in front of the house.

Ryan headed for the house. Shandra put a hand on his arm and pointed to the barn.

"Lil lives in the barn. That's where she'd be."

Ryan changed directions and crept to the back of the barn.

Light shimmered in the tack room window. But it was too high to see into. Shandra moved past Ryan to the small door in the back of the barn. Lil kept things well maintained. Shandra knew the door wouldn't creak or squeak and give away their approach.

They both slipped into the barn and edged toward the tack room.

Voices drifted into the darkness.

"I told Mommy you wouldn't be able to make him go away."

Shandra put a hand on Ryan's arm. She didn't recognize the female voice.

"Janine, what are you talking about?" Lil asked, her voice a bit shaky.

"When I called Mommy and told her Johnny was flashing a ring and going to ask you to marry him, she said she'd send Jerome to buy him off." Janine's voice was rising in pitch.

"Lil, I'm sorry, but Aunt May wanted the

ranch." Jerome said. "We knew about the trust, and she wanted me to pay Johnny to leave."

"You offered Johnny money to not marry me? But why did you kill him?" Lil's voice came out low and hard.

"I didn't kill him. When he refused to take the money, I went down to Gran and Pappy and tried to persuade them to not let you marry him." He shook his head. "That's when I saw you come out of the barn and it caught fire."

"That wasn't me! I told you that back then and I'm telling you now." Lil's voice rose as she enunciated each word. "I. Did. Not. Set. Fire. To. The. Barn."

A feminine cackle chilled the air. "No, it wasn't sweet Lil. I was the one who set fire to the barn. I followed you to the mountain, heard Johnny refuse to leave Lil. When you left, I strolled up and asked him why he was waiting on the mountain. He said he'd left a note for Lil in the barn to come to him. He said he planned to camp on the mountain until she arrived. I found out what part of the barn he'd left the note. When he turned away from me and reached down to pick up a jacket on the ground, I hit him in the head with a limb I'd picked up on the way up the trail."

Lil gasped.

Shandra gripped Ryan's arm. Janine told the story so coldly, shivers slithered through Shandra's bones.

"But how did my key chain get under Johnny?" *Good question, Lil.* Shandra smiled at the woman's quick mind even though she had to be torn up hearing how her lover died.

"I left him there. Ran down the trail back to the house. I set the barn on fire, stole the keys from your truck, and brought a shovel back up. I dug the hole, dropped the keys in, and shoved Johnny in."

Shandra couldn't stand it any longer she had to know what the situation was in the room. It wouldn't be unusual for her to walk into her own barn. She'd leave Ryan out here to charge to the rescue.

She shoved the door open. A tug on her shirt revealed Ryan wasn't happy with her decision. "Then how did your mother get the ring Johnny was going to give to Lil?"

Janine pivoted toward her with a gun in her hand. Lil and Jerome sat duct taped to chairs.

"One more to burn in an accidental barn fire." Janine motioned with the revolver for Shandra to move over next to the other two.

Shandra moved slowly, keeping her gaze on the crazy woman with the gun. "You didn't answer my question. How did your mother get the ring?" She had to keep the woman's attention so Ryan could apprehend her.

"I took it and had a jeweler erase the last part of Johnny's name. I gave it to Mommy and told her she wouldn't have to worry about Johnny."

The pride in Janine's voice made Shandra shudder.

"She told us your father gave her the ring."

Janine sneered. "That's because dear daddy is leaving a note. He's sorry for killing Johnny and couldn't live with himself."

"How were you going to explain my death alongside my uncle?" Lil asked.

"He wanted you to finally be with Johnny. He's crazy you know, just like you." Janine's gaze flitted to each of her captives.

Shandra had a good idea who was the real crazy person in the room.

Lewis strolled into the room, meowing. He wound around Lil's feet and jumped into her lap. Her hands were tied and she couldn't pet him.

Different scenarios ran through Shandra's mind. She latched on to the easiest one. With one quick motion, she picked up the orange cat, ruffling his hair. He hated his hair roughed up. His ears laid back and his eyes grew wider.

"The only person in this family that's crazy is you," Shandra said, tossing the cat at the woman and shouting. "Now!"

Lewis hissed and hit Janine in the chest.

Janine dropped the gun, flailing her arms.

Lewis landed on his feet and ran over to hide behind Lil's legs.

Ryan hurtled through the door and grasped Janine, yanking her arms behind her back. Shandra searched the room for a knife to cut Lil and her uncle free.

Chapter Twenty-nine

The clock on the oven clicked over to midnight. Shandra handed Lil a glass of wine and a beer to Lil's uncle. Ryan walked through the door. She pivoted back to the refrigerator and plucked a beer for Ryan. The stubble on his face, wrinkled clothes, and droopy eyelids proved he was ready to finish the day.

After detaining Janine, Ryan had called for backup to take her to jail and to help take statements. May had arrived at this point, shouting obscenities at her husband and accusing him of killing Johnny, not Janine. The sheriff's department cars finally left, taking Janine and May with them.

Shandra wanted to feel sorry for the mother and daughter, but she couldn't. They'd considered their own wealth over that of the life of another. And the irony, after killing Johnny, the ranch was sold and the only way they could get it was to purchase it. Something neither wanted to do with the body on the mountain.

Jerome put a hand over Lil's resting on the counter. "I'm sorry for all the sorrow my family brought you. I didn't have a clue about what they did. But when you called today and started asking questions, I had to come see you and figure out what was happening."

Lil smiled at her uncle. "It's okay. Now that I know Johnny didn't desert me, I feel free." She shook her head. "Don't get me wrong, I want them punished for his death, but I know he didn't leave because he wanted to."

Her dreamy gaze and wistful smile brought a lump to Shandra's throat.

"Janine will go to prison for sure. Her mother is an accessory." Ryan took a sip of beer. "Robert just called and said it looked like the mother was turning on the daughter."

Jerome snorted. "May has always been out for herself. I could see her turning on Janine to keep herself out of jail. Poor Janine was just a pawn in May's game of trying to gather the most of everything." He shook his head and peered at Lil. "I'm sorry for all those years they told people you were crazy. It was those two who were crazy."

"Why did you stay with Aunt May?" Lil asked. "I could tell years ago you two weren't happy."

"Her money started my hardware store. And kept it open when times were bad. She threatened to take it away if I strayed or left her. It was all I had after the ranch sold. I'd wanted that ranch so I'd have my own financial independence, but Lil, I would have never killed for it. When I saw how much Johnny loved you by turning down the fifty-thousand May sent me to offer him, I decided to try other tactics."

"Like getting Lil thrown in jail for arson and then spreading rumors she was unfit to take over the ranch?" Shandra wasn't going to soften to the man who could and should have stood up for Lil all those years.

He had the decency to blush. "When I saw the barn on fire and saw a young woman with blonde hair running from the barn, I thought it was Lil."

"You didn't even recognize your own daughter?" Ryan spoke up.

Jerome shrugged. "Step-daughter. I thought it was Janine at first, but she wasn't supposed to be there, so I figured it had to be Lil. At the time, from a distance, they were hard to tell apart. Especially from the back."

Shandra had a question that had been nudging the back of her mind for hours. "What I don't understand is how quickly Janine, and even you, made it up and down the mountain from the murder site, my clay pocket? It takes me hours on a horse to make that trek."

Lil sat up. "Thirty years ago there was a direct trail to that spot from the back of the barn up through the rocks. Pappy said it was made by Indians who would go up beyond the clay pocket to watch for intruders. It could only take foot traffic because it's narrow and carved in the rocks. Someone in good shape can climb it easy in an hour. The trail we made for you for the horses takes longer because we have to switch back and find paths wide enough for a horse with a pack."

Ryan perked up. "Is the trail still navigable?"

Lil shook her head. "I don't think anyone has used it for years. Once Johnny was gone, I had no reason to go to that spot. The first time I'd been there in decades was when Shandra found the clay and insisted on a trail to get to it."

Jerome stood. "I better get back to Hafersville and see what I need to do about my wife and Janine."

"You're not going to stand by them knowing what they did?" Shandra knew family stuck together, but she'd never condone a family member murdering someone.

"I need to see they have attorneys. After that, they're on their own. I'll have enough fallout at the store when this hits the news. I don't need to be siding with them or I'll lose everything for sure." He turned to Lil. "Again, I'm sorry my family cost you a happy future."

Lil stood and hugged Jerome. "I still have you." She released the man.

When Jerome turned, Shandra saw tears glistening in his eyes.

"Good-night," Shandra said, walking him to the door.

"Drive safe," Ryan said from behind her.

Shandra shut the door on Jerome and faced Ryan.

"That was a fool-hardy thing you did tonight." His voice was stern, but his gaze fluctuated between her eyes and her lips.

"We didn't know what was going on in that room. We could have stood out there for an hour and discovered they were just talking. We had to know if there was a weapon involved." She'd wondered when he would take her to task for running into the tack room.

"And then throwing a cat at a woman with a gun…" He backed her up against the door. "You could have been killed. She could have fired at the cat and you would have been in the line of the bullet."

"The way her hand was wobbling while holding the gun, I didn't think she even knew how to shoot it. But I needed a distraction so you could apprehend her." Shandra's heart was racing as Ryan pushed closer.

"Standing outside that door, waiting and listening." He released a long drawn out breath. "My heart stopped twice imagining that woman shooting you. And like a bad dream, me getting to you too late."

Shandra stared at the snaps on his shirt. If she looked into his eyes she'd say something like, I promise to never do that again. And she'd never be able to keep that promise if someone she cared about was in danger again.

Ryan tucked a finger under her chin and raised her face. She peered into his dark, brown concerned eyes.

"Promise—"

"Shandra, I'm headed to bed," Lil's voice called from the kitchen.

Gah! She'd forgotten they weren't alone. Shandra ducked around Ryan and briskly walked into the kitchen. She crossed the room and hugged Lil.

"After tonight, I think you deserve a good night's sleep. See you in the morning." She released the woman and watched her walk out the door.

Strong arms circled her. "You don't have anyone left to get you out of promising me you'll stop running head long into trouble." Ryan's voice was warm against her ear.

"I can't promise you that. If someone I care about is in trouble, I have to help." She remained wrapped in his arms, enjoying the feeling of security he evoked.

"Then if you must help, call me for back up."

She spun in his arms. "I think that is a very good idea, Detective." Half circles darkened the skin beneath his eyes. "I say you need a good night's sleep. That guest room is yours whenever you need it."

He raised an eyebrow. "I'll take that offer tonight." He dipped his face down and kissed her.

When her toes were curling from the heat of the kiss, he released her lips and her body.

"I'll see you in the morning." Ryan walked to the door of the guest room and disappeared.

Shandra smiled. Today they'd discovered the true killer of Johnny Clark, and Lil now knew she was loved. She glanced at the guest room door. I have a feeling I've found my Johnny Clark. But time will tell.

Book Three in the Shandra Higheagle Mystery
Series:

Deadly Aim

Chapter One

Shandra Higheagle watched her bear-sized dog
lope off through the huckleberry bushes this
mountain was named for. Sheba loved lumbering
over the mountain while Shandra rode her horse.
This was Shandra's favorite time of the year to ride.
The changing colors and brisk air autumn air
energized.

Lil, Shandra's Jill-of-all-trades had suggested
the ride. After a two-week sojourn to teaching and
displaying her pottery at an art show in New
Mexico, Shandra needed a leisurely horseback ride
to get back in tune with nature. Every time she
spent more than a few days off the mountain she
had to get reacquainted with her roots in order to re-
submerge herself in her art.

But it wasn't just her time away that had her
mind wandering. Only one more week and she'd be
attending Ryan's brother's wedding to Ryan's ex-
girlfriend. She and the handsome Weippe detective
hadn't made any kind of commitment to one
another, but she did find his company pleasurable.
And she had to admit she was curious about his
family and the woman who he'd set his sights on
marrying in seventh grade.

"Woof! Woof!"

Sheba's excited bark caught Shandra's
attention. It didn't sound like her pursuing or scared
bark. It had a mournful lilt to it.

"Where are you, girl?" Shandra stood in the stirrups and scanned the area she'd last seen her dog. Her gelding, Apple, started dancing nervously and he blew air in short snorts. Something had both animals on alert.

"Woof! Woof!"

She zeroed in on the sound and reined Apple that direction. Sheba's head was down and the way her body shook, she was digging.

"What is it girl?" Shandra dodged a tree limb as Apple snorted and started to back up.

"Whoa. What has you spooked?" She ran a hand down the horse's neck to soothe him and stared at the ground where Sheba pawed.

Her stomach lurched and her mouth went dry. Sheba dug at the ground next to a bloody, disemboweled body.

She pivoted Apple and sat with her back to the sight. "Sheba, come!" she ordered without glancing back. When Sheba appeared beside the horse, Shandra leaned down and patted the dog on the head. "Good girl. Stay."

She straightened in the saddle and the image flashed in her mind. "Why do I find all the bodies on this mountain?"

The small bar on her phone faded in and out. "I have to give it a try. I don't want to leave this poor person to any more animals." She found Ryan's name and pushed the dial button.

"Shandra, I…thinking…you."

His voice cutting in and out wasn't a good sign.

"I found a body. Go to my ranch and have Lil

bring you out to me." She hoped he heard enough to know what to do.

"Body? Are… How…" The connection broke.

She took a deep breath trying to decide how to keep the body from being eaten by any more animals. She couldn't leave Sheba. The dog's size would be daunting for most animals but if an animal so much as growled, she'd be back at the ranch faster than a jet.

Her phone beeped.

Glancing at the front she spotted a text message.

Where R you? Ryan asked.

She typed back. *Found body along east property line. Lil can bring you.*

K, he text in reply.

Now to spend two hours waiting for them without looking at the body. Who could this be and why were they on my property? She tied Apple to a tree, sat down on a log, and hugged Sheba. I've never felt scared on the mountain before.

~*~

Ryan was a half hour from Huckleberry and then another forty-five minutes from Shandra's ranch. He was beginning to think the woman was a body detector. First the gallery owner, then the thirty-year-old skeleton, and who knew what she'd stumbled across this time. The only thing he did know—he'd always be there for the eccentric artist. The past few months he'd spent more and more time with the woman. The more he learned about her, he knew she was the one that when he was ready to settle down, he'd ask her to marry him.

With lights flashing and sirens blaring he swerved off Hwy 90, turned right and barreled down the main street of Huckleberry. The ritzy resort had been off-limits to a sheep rancher's son growing up forty miles away, but now it was part of his territory as a Weippe County Detective.

No sooner had he entered and exited town than he was flying at eighty miles an hour up the county road toward Shandra's ranch. The woman liked living on her mountain. The more he visited her there, the more he understood how the area revitalized and fed her artistic talents. Part of his speed was to find the body, but the other part was the fact Shandra had been gone for two weeks. He'd told himself he'd give her a couple days to recuperate then invite himself to dinner. He'd never planned on seeing her again because of a dead body.

He whipped his SUV up a side road nearly hidden by overgrown pines. This bumpy miserable excuse for a road was Shandra's way of keeping people out. It looked like a forest service road and not vehicle friendly. He had to slow the Tahoe to a crawl to navigate the bumps and not toss all his equipment in the back into a heap. The house, studio, and barn came into view and he understood Shandra's penchant for not wanting to leave her place.

His siren still blared as Lil, Shandra's employee, walked out of the barn with the old orange cat wrapped around her neck like a live fur stole. The woman wore her signature purple clothing. Today it was an over-sized sweatshirt and stocking cap. Her gray hair stuck out like spikes on a flail.

He braked in front of the barn, shut off the lights and siren, and hopped out of the vehicle. "Shandra called. She's found another body."

Lil shook her head. "What is with that woman?"

"My thoughts exactly." Ryan strode toward the barn with Lil beside him. "She said it was along the east property line and you'd know how to get me there."

Lil nodded and pointed to the gelding Ryan rode when he and Shandra trail rode together.

He walked to the stall. "Hey, Duke. We're after another body, you game?" He led the horse out and had him saddled by the time Lil swung up into the saddle of her horse.

"Is the east property line very far?" He wondered about logistics to get the coroner and other deputies to the site.

"About an hour. If she said I knew where she was, then she's on her usual route for a trail ride." Lil nudged her horse, and they trotted into the trees.

I might as well gather information. "Who owns the land bordering Shandra on the east?"

"J.W. Randal."

He wished he could pull out his notebook and jot that down but the trail so far was fairly smooth and Lil kept the gait at a trot.

"Big land owner or a seasonal resident?"

"Land owner."

Lil was always one for few words but he'd like some elaboration. "What does he use the land for?"

Lil slowed her horse and stared at him. "Cattle and big game hunting."

She said the last with contempt.

"He has the required license to do big game hunts?" Randal. The name was familiar. Where had he heard it? He'd tried to learn all the licensed big game hunting reserves.

"All I know is people pay lots of money to shoot animals on his place. He was in the paper a few weeks ago for using illegal tags."

About the Author

Award-winning author Paty Jager and her husband raise alfalfa hay in rural eastern Oregon. On her road to publication she wrote freelance articles for two local newspapers and enjoyed her job with the County Extension service as a 4-H Program Assistant. Raising hay and cattle, riding horses, and battling rattlesnakes, she not only writes the western lifestyle, she lives it.

http://www.patyjager.net

More Shandra Higheagle Mysteries

Double Duplicity
Tarnished Remains
Deadly Aim
Murderous Secrets
Killer Descent

Thank you for purchasing this Windtree Press
publication. For other books of the heart, please
visit our website at www.windtreepress.com.

For questions or more information contact us at
info@windtreepress.com.

Windtree Press
www.windtreepress.com